MODERN SHORT STORIES

NOVELS BY JIM HUNTER

Kinship
Percival And The Presence Of God

EDITED BY JIM HUNTER

Modern Poets 1–4

MODERN
SHORT STORIES

★

*edited
with an introduction
and notes by*

JIM HUNTER
(Headmaster, Weymouth Grammar School)

FABER AND FABER
LONDON . BOSTON

First published in 1964
by Faber and Faber Limited
3 Queen Square London WC1
Reprinted 1966, 1967, 1968 (three times),
1969 (twice), 1970, 1971, 1972, 1973 (twice)
Reset and reprinted 1974 and 1975 (twice)
Reprinted 1977, 1979 and 1981
Printed in Great Britain by
Fakenham Press Limited, Fakenham, Norfolk
All rights reserved

ISBN 0 571 08744 2 (paper covers)

CONTENTS

★

5

Contents

INTRODUCTION

★

This is a selection of short stories written in English during the last forty-odd years. Naturally enough, it is a personal one; I have put in what I like, and excluded one or two common modern types which I dislike, in particular the slick, bloodless, magazine story which depends for its appeal not upon any real concern, or warmth, or honesty, but upon either a "twist", an unexpected and "ironic" ending, or upon a brilliant recording of the talk of talkative (and often bored) people. In general, however, this is a fairly representative selection of modern short stories, some of them by famous authors, some not; some good writers have been left out, but this was inevitable in such a comparatively rich field.

A majority of the writers who appear here are dead, and their fame is firmly established; yet I am constantly surprised to meet people who are frightened or embarrassed when one or another such writer is mentioned: they regard him as dangerously "modern". I hope this book will reassure such readers, and encourage them to do the "catching-up" which they will enjoy. To this end, the notes to most stories include some recommendations to further reading, and I hope these will prove useful.

There is little point in my making generalizations here about the short story or about modern fiction. All that needs to be said is that we should appreciate the immense variety, of mood and of form, which we are offered; and that our judgment should be made not according to any "rules", but according to the result. How does it work for me? What do

I gain from reading this? Is the humour, or the brevity, or the complexity, or the violence, justified, when one looks back? In fiction, as in everything really important, there are no rules; every success is a sort of break-through, beyond what is systematic or predictable. I have made some comments of my own in the notes which accompany each story; and these, often in the form of questions, are meant to direct attention to particular strengths, and special implications, rather than to present placing judgments.

Most readers will probably prefer to read the stories silently; but often this can be followed by group discussion, more or less guided by a teacher, and the re-reading together of certain parts. The tendency in the book is for the more testing stories to appear later; but there is certainly no need to read the stories in the order printed, or, indeed, to read every one of them. My main hope is that of any editor: that they will please, and hold the interest.

One more word, particularly to the young readers, about fourteen years old and upwards, for whom this book is primarily intended. All these stories, even the humorous ones, are of an adult kind; they have been chosen for you, but not softened or thinned down. In many of them death, or pain, or love, are strongly and honestly treated; and I have put them in this book because I believe that in the long run you will prefer strength, even if it involves some difficulty, to a flimsy glitter; and honesty, to the comfortable falsifications which are today being offered regularly to children and—still worse—to adults. The writers in this book do not intend to drug their readers, or soothe them, in any way, but to delight and disturb; in return for this they expect your respect, your wits, and your lively sympathy.

8

DYLAN THOMAS

Dylan Thomas was a Welshman who died in 1953 at the age of thirty-nine. He is one of the most popular poets and story-tellers of the century, and his reputation has been highest since his death, though it is probably now declining. His main characteristic is a bewildering excitability of language, which, with greater sureness of intention and control, might have made him an important poet; as it is, I feel that he is at his best when less pretentious, an entertainer with far more vitality than most. You will see this talent in *The Peaches*; here Thomas's enthusiasm for pushing words around is saved from pointlessness by his keen memory of what it was really like to be a young schoolboy. Few writers have done this so well.

The Peaches

The grass-green cart, with "J. Jones, Gorsehill" painted shakily on it, stopped in the cobblestone passage between "The Hare's Foot" and "The Pure Drop". It was late on an April evening. Uncle Jim, in his black collar, loud new boots, and a plaid cap, creaked and climbed down. He dragged out a thick wicker basket from a heap of straw in the corner of the cart and swung it over his shoulder. I heard a squeal from the basket and saw the tip of a pink tail curling out as Uncle Jim opened the public door of "The Pure Drop".

"I won't be two minutes," he said to me. The bar was full; two fat women in bright dresses sat near the door, one with a small, dark child on her knee; they saw Uncle Jim and nudged up on the bench.

"I'll be out straight away," he said fiercely, as though I had contradicted him, "you stay there quiet."

The woman without the child raised up her hands. "Oh, Mr. Jones," she said in a high laughing voice. She shook like a jelly.

Then the door closed and the voices were muffled.

I sat alone on the shaft of the cart in the narrow passage, staring through a side window of "The Hare's Foot". A stained blind was drawn half over it. I could see into half of a smoky, secret room, where four men were playing cards. One man was huge and swarthy, with a handlebar moustache and a love-curl on his forehead; seated by his side was a thin, bald, pale old man with his cheeks in his mouth; the faces of the other two were in shadow. They all drank out of brown pint tankards and never spoke, laying the cards down with a smack, scraping at their matchboxes, puffing at their pipes, swallowing unhappily, ringing the brass bell, ordering more, by a sign of the fingers, from a sour woman with a flowered blouse and a man's cap.

The passage grew dark too suddenly, the walls crowded in, and the roofs crouched down. To me, staring timidly there in a dark passage in a strange town, the swarthy man appeared like a giant in a cage surrounded by clouds, and the bald old man withered into a black hump with a white top; two white hands darted out of the corner with invisible cards. A man with spring-heeled boots and a two-edged knife might be bouncing towards me from Union Street.

10

I called, "Uncle Jim, Uncle Jim," softly so that he should not hear.

I began to whistle between my teeth, but when I stopped I thought the sound went hissing on behind me. I climbed down the shaft and stepped close to the half-blind window; a hand clawed up the pane to the tassel of the blind; in the little, packed space between me on the cobbles and the card-players at the table, I could not tell which side of the glass was the hand that dragged the blind down slowly. I was cut from the night by a stained square. A story I had made in the warm, safe island of my bed, with sleepy midnight Swansea flowing and rolling round outside the house, came blowing down to me then with a noise on the cobbles. I remembered the demon in the story, with his wings and hooks, who clung like a bat to my hair as I battled up and down Wales after a tall, wise, golden, royal girl from Swansea Convent. I tried to remember her true name, her proper, long, black-stockinged legs, her giggle and paper curls, but the hooked wings tore at me and the colour of her hair and eyes faded and vanished like the grass-green of the cart that was a dark, grey mountain now standing between the passage walls.

And all this time the old, broad, patient, nameless mare stood without stirring, not stamping once on the cobbles or shaking her reins. I called her a good girl and stood on tiptoe to try to stroke her ears as the door of "The Pure Drop" swung open and the warm lamplight from the bar dazzled me and burned my story up. I felt frightened no longer, only angry and hungry. The two fat women near the door giggled "Good night, Mr. Jones" out of the rich noise and the comfortable smells. The child lay curled asleep under the bench. Uncle Jim kissed the two women on the lips.

"Good night."

"Good night."

"Good night."

Then the passage was dark again.

He backed the mare into Union Street, lurching against her side, cursing her patience and patting her nose, and we both climbed into the cart.

"There are too many drunken gipsies," he said as we rolled and rattled through the flickering, lamp-lit town.

He sang hymns all the way to Gorsehill in an affectionate bass voice, and conducted the wind with his whip. He did not need to touch the reins. Once on the rough road, between hedges twisting out to twig the mare by the bridle and poke our caps, we stopped, at a whispered "Whoa", for uncle to light his pipe and set the darkness on fire and show his long, red, drunken, fox's face to me, with its bristling side-bushes and wet, sensitive nose. A white house with a light in one bedroom window shone in a field on a short hill beyond the road.

Uncle whispered, "Easy, easy, girl," to the mare, though she was standing calmly, and said to me over his shoulder in a suddenly loud voice: "A hangman lived there."

He stamped on the shaft, and we rattled on through a cutting wind. Uncle shivered, pulling down his cap to hide his ears; but the mare was like a clumsy statue trotting, and all the demons of my stories, if they trotted by her side or crowded together and grinned into her eyes, would not make her shake her head or hurry.

"I wish he'd have hung Mrs. Jesus," uncle said.

Between hymns he cursed the mare in Welsh. The white house was left behind, the light and the hill were swallowed up.

"Nobody lives there now," he said.

We drove into the farmyard of Gorsehill, where the cobbles rang and the black, empty stables took up the ringing and hollowed it so that we drew up in a hollow circle of darkness and the mare was a hollow animal and nothing lived in the hollow house at the end of the yard but two sticks with faces scooped out of turnips.

"You run and see Annie," said uncle. "There'll be hot broth and potatoes."

He led the hollow, shaggy statue towards the stable; clop, clop to the mice-house. I heard locks rattle as I ran to the farmhouse door.

The front of the house was the single side of a black shell, and the arched door was the listening ear. I pushed the door open and walked into the passage out of the wind. I might have been walking into the hollow night and the wind, passing through a tall vertical shell on an inland sea-shore. Then a door at the end of the passage opened; I saw the plates on the shelves, the lighted lamp on the long, oil-clothed table, "Prepare to Meet Thy God" knitted over the fire-place, the smiling china dogs, the brown-stained settle, the grandmother clock, and I ran into the kitchen and into Annie's arms.

There was a welcome, then. The clock struck twelve as she kissed me, and I stood among the shining and striking like a prince taking off his disguise. One minute I was small and cold, skulking dead-scared down a black passage in my stiff, best suit, with my hollow belly thumping and my heart like a time bomb, clutching my grammar school cap, unfamiliar to myself, a snub-nosed story-teller lost in his own adventures and longing to be home; the next I was a royal nephew in smart town clothes, embraced and welcomed, standing in the snug centre of my stories and listening to the clock announcing me. She hurried me to the seat in the side of the cavernous fire-place and took off my shoes. The bright lamps and the ceremonial gongs blazed and rang for me.

She made a mustard bath and strong tea, told me to put on a pair of my cousin Gwilym's socks and an old coat of uncle's that smelt of rabbit and tobacco. She fussed and clucked and nodded and told me, as she cut bread and butter, how Gwilym was still studying to be a minister, and how Aunt Rach Morgan, who was ninety years old, had fallen on her belly on a scythe.

Then Uncle Jim came in like the devil with a red face and a wet nose and trembling, hairy hands. His walk was thick. He stumbled against the dresser and shook the coronation plates, and a lean cat shot booted out from the settle corner. Uncle looked nearly twice as tall as Annie. He could have carried her about under his coat and brought her out suddenly, a little, brown-skinned, toothless, hunchbacked woman with a cracked, sing-song voice.

"You shouldn't have kept him out so long," she said, angry and timid.

He sat down in his special chair, which was the broken throne of a bankrupt bard, and lit his pipe and stretched his legs and puffed clouds at the ceiling.

"He might catch his death of cold," she said.

She talked at the back of his head while he wrapped himself in clouds. The cat slunk back. I sat at the table with my supper finished, and found a little empty bottle in the pockets of my coat.

"Run off to bed, there's a dear," Annie whispered.

"Can I go and look at the pigs?"

"In the morning, dear," she said.

So I said good night to Uncle Jim, who turned and smiled at me and winked through the smoke, and I kissed Annie and lit my candle.

"Good night."

"Good night."

"Good night."

I climbed the stairs; each had a different voice. The house smelt of rotten wood and damp and animals. I thought that I had been walking long, damp passages all my life, and climbing stairs in the dark, alone. I stopped outside Gwilym's door on the draughty landing.

"Good night."

The candle flame jumped in my bedroom where a lamp was burning very low, and the curtains waved; the water in a glass on a round table by the bed stirred, I thought, as the door closed, and lapped against the sides. There was a stream below the window; I thought it lapped against the house all night until I slept.

"Can I go and see the pigs?" I asked Gwilym next morning. The hollow fear of the house was gone, and, running downstairs to my breakfast, I smelt the sweetness of wood and the fresh spring grass and the quiet untidy farmyard, with its tumbledown dirty-white cowhouse and empty stables open.

Gwilym was a tall young man aged nearly twenty, with a thin stick of a body and spade-shaped face. You could dig the garden with him. He had a deep voice that cracked in half when he was excited, and he sang songs to himself, treble and bass, with the same sad hymn tune, and wrote hymns in the barn. He told me stories about girls who died for love. "And she put a rope round a tree but it was too short," he said; "she stuck a pen-knife in her bosoms but it was too blunt." We were sitting together on the straw heaps that day in the half dark of the shuttered stable. He twisted and leaned near to me, raising his big finger, and the straw creaked.

"She jumped in the cold river, she jumped," he said, his mouth against my ear, "and, Diu, she was dead." He squeaked like a bat.

The pigsties were at the far end of the yard. We walked towards them, Gwilym dressed in minister's black, though it was a week-day morning, and me in a serge suit with a darned bottom, past three hens scrabbling the muddy cobbles and a collie with one eye, sleeping with it open. The ramshackle outhouses had tumbling, rotten roofs, jagged holes in their

15

sides, broken shutters, and peeling whitewash; rusty screws ripped out from the dangling, crooked boards; the lean cat of the night before sat snugly between the splintered jaws of bottles, cleaning its face, on the tip of the rubbish pile that rose triangular and smelling sweet and strong to the level of the riddled carthouse roof. There was nowhere like that farmyard in all the slapdash county, nowhere so poor and grand and dirty as that square of mud and rubbish and bad wood and falling stone, where a bucketful of old and bedraggled hens scratched and laid small eggs. A duck quacked out of the trough in one deserted sty. Now a young man and a curly boy stood staring and sniffing over a wall at a sow, with its tits on the mud, giving suck.

"How many pigs are there?"

"Five. The bitch ate one," said Gwilym.

We counted them as they squirmed and wriggled, rolled on their backs and bellies, edged and pinched and pushed and squealed about their mother. There were four. We counted again. Four pigs, four naked pink tails curling up as their mouths guzzled down and the sow grunted with pain and joy.

"She must have ate another," I said, and picked up a scratching-stick and prodded the grunting sow and rubbed her crusted bristles backwards. "Or a fox jumped over the wall," I said.

"It wasn't the sow or the fox," said Gwilym. "It was father."

I could see uncle, tall and sly and red, holding the writhing pig in his two hairy hands, sinking his teeth in its thigh, crunching its trotters up; I could see him leaning over the wall of the sty with the pig's legs sticking out of his mouth, "Did Uncle Jim eat the pig?"

Now, at this minute, behind the rotting sheds, he was standing, knee-deep in feathers, chewing off the live heads of the poultry.

"He sold it to go on the drink," said Gwilym in his deepest

rebuking whisper, his eyes fixed on the sky. "Last Christmas he took a sheep over his shoulder, and he was drunk for ten days."

The sow rolled nearer the scratching-stick, and the small pigs sucking at her, lost and squealing in the sudden darkness, struggled under her folds and pouches.

"Come and see my chapel," said Gwilym. He forgot the lost pig at once and began to talk about the towns he had visited on a religious tour, Neath and Bridgend and Bristol and Newport, with their lakes and luxury gardens, their bright, coloured streets roaring with temptation. We walked away from the sty and the disappointed sow.

"I met actress after actress," he said.

Gwilym's chapel was the last old barn before the field that led down to the river; it stood well above the farmyard, on a mucky hill. There was one whole door with a heavy padlock, but you could get in easily through the holes on either side of it. He took out a ring of keys and shook them gently and tried each one in the lock. "Very posh," he said; "I bought them from the junk-shop in Carmarthen." We climbed into the chapel through a hole.

A dusty wagon with the name painted out and a whitewash cross on its side stood in the middle. "My pulpit cart," he said, and walked solemnly into it up the broken shaft. "You sit on the hay; mind the mice," he said. Then he brought out his deepest voice again and cried to the heavens and the bat-lined rafters and the hanging webs: "Bless us this holy day, O Lord, bless me and Dylan and this Thy little chapel for ever and ever, Amen. I've done a lot of improvements to this place."

I sat on the hay and stared at Gwilym preaching, and heard his voice rise and crack and sink to a whisper and break into singing and Welsh and ring triumphantly and be wild and meek. The sun, through a hole, shone on his praying shoulders, and he said: "O God, Thou art everywhere all the time, in the dew of the morning, in the frost of the evening, in the field and the town, in the preacher and sinner, in the sparrow and the big buzzard. Thou canst see everything, right down deep in our hearts; Thou canst see us when the sun is gone; Thou canst see us when there aren't any stars, in the gravy blackness, in the deep, deep, deep, deep pit; Thou canst see and spy and watch us all the time, in the little black corners, in the big cowboys' prairies, under the blankets when we're snoring fast, in the terrible shadows, pitch black, pitch black; Thou canst see everything we do, in the night and the day, in the day and the night, everything, everything; Thou canst see all the time. O God, mun, you're like a bloody cat."

He let his clasped hands fall. The chapel in the barn was still, and shafted with sunlight. There was nobody to cry Hallelujah or God-bless; I was too small and enamoured in the silence. The one duck quacked outside.

"Now I take a collection," Gwilym said.

He stepped down from the cart and groped about in the hay beneath it and held out a battered tin to me.

"I haven't got a proper box," he said.

I put two pennies in the tin.

"It's time for dinner," he said, and we went back to the house without a word.

Annie said, when we had finished dinner: "Put on your nice suit for this afternoon. The one with stripes."

It was to be a special afternoon, for my best friend, Jack Williams, from Swansea, was coming down with his rich mother in a motor-car, and Jack was to spend a fortnight's holiday with me.

"Where's Uncle Jim?"

"He's gone to market," said Annie.

Gwilym made a small pig's noise. We knew where uncle was; he was sitting in a public house with a heifer over his shoulders and two pigs nosing out of his pockets, and his lips were wet with bull's blood.

"Is Mrs. Williams very rich?" asked Gwilym.

I told him she had three motor-cars and two houses, which was a lie. "She's the richest woman in Wales, and once she was a mayoress," I said. "Are we going to have tea in the best room?"

Annie nodded. "And a large tin of peaches," she said.

"That old tin's been in the cupboard since Christmas," said Gwilym, "mother's been keeping it for a day like this."

"They're lovely peaches," Annie said. She went upstairs to dress like Sunday.

The best room smelt of moth-balls and fur and damp and dead plants and stale, sour air. Two glass cases on wooden coffin-boxes lined the window wall. You looked at the weed-grown vegetable garden through a stuffed fox's legs, over a partridge's head, along the red-paint-stained breast of a stiff wild duck. A case of china and pewter, trinkets, teeth, family brooches, stood beyond the bandy table; there was a large oil-lamp on the patchwork tablecloth, a Bible with a clasp, a tall vase with a draped woman about to bathe on it, and a framed photograph of Annie, Uncle Jim, and Gwilym smiling in front of a fern-pot. On the mantelpiece were two clocks, some dogs, brass candlesticks, a shepherdess, a man in a kilt, and a tinted photograph of Annie, with high hair and her breasts coming out. There were chairs around the table and in each corner, straight, curved, stained, padded, all with lace cloths hanging over their backs. A patched white sheet shrouded the harmonium. The fire-place was full of brass tongs, shovels, and pokers. The best room was rarely used. Annie dusted and brushed and polished there once a week, but the carpet still sent up a grey cloud when you trod on it, and dust lay evenly on the seats of the chairs, and balls of cotton and dirt and black stuffing and long black horse hairs were wedged in the cracks of the sofa. I blew on the glass to see pictures. Gwilym and castles and cattle.

"Change your suit now," said Gwilym.

I wanted to wear my old suit, to look like a proper farm boy and have manure in my shoes and hear it squelch as I walked, to see a cow have calves, to run down in the dingle and wet my stockings, to go out and shout, "Come on, you b——," and pelt the hens and talk in a proper voice. But I went upstairs to put my striped suit on.

From my bedroom I heard the noise of a motor-car drawing up in the yard. It was Jack Williams and his mother.

Gwilym shouted, "They're here, in a Daimler!" from the foot of the stairs, and I ran down to meet them with my tie undone and my hair uncombed.

Annie was saying at the door: "Good afternoon, Mrs. Williams, good afternoon. Come right in, it's a lovely day, Mrs. Williams. Did you have a nice journey then? This way, Mrs. Williams, mind the step."

Annie wore a black, shining dress that smelt of moth-balls, like the chair covers in the best room; she had forgotten to change her gym shoes, which were caked with mud and all holes. She fussed on before Mrs. Williams down the stone passage, darting her head round, clucking, fidgeting, excusing the small house, anxiously tidying her hair with one rough, stubby hand.

Mrs. Williams was tall and stout, with a jutting bosom and thick legs, her ankles swollen over her pointed shoes; she was fitted out like a mayoress or a ship, and she swayed after Annie into the best room.

She said: "Please don't put yourself out for me, Mrs. Jones, there's a dear." She dusted the seat of a chair with a lace handkerchief from her bag before sitting down.

"I can't stop, you know," she said.

"Oh, you must stay for a cup of tea," said Annie, shifting

and scraping the chairs away from the table so that nobody could move and Mrs. Williams was hemmed in fast with her bosom and her rings and her bag, opening the china cupboard, upsetting the Bible on the floor, picking it up, dusting it hurriedly with her sleeve.

"And peaches," Gwilym said. He was standing in the passage with his hat on.

Annie said, "Take your hat off, Gwilym, make Mrs. Williams comfortable," and she put the lamp on the shrouded harmonium and spread out a white table-cloth that had a tea stain in the centre, and brought out the china and laid knives and cups for five.

"Don't bother about me, there's a dear," said Mrs. Williams. "There's a lovely fox!" She flashed a finger of rings at the glass case.

"It's real blood," I told Jack, and we climbed over the sofa to the table.

"No, it isn't," he said, "it's red ink."

"Oh, your shoes!" said Annie.

"Don't tread on the sofa, Jack, there's a dear."

"If it isn't ink it's paint then."

Gwilym said: "Shall I get you a bit of cake, Mrs. Williams?"

Annie rattled the tea-cups. "There isn't a single bit of cake in the house," she said; "we forgot to order it from the shop; not a single bit. Oh, Mrs. Williams!"

Mrs. Williams said: "Just a cup of tea, thanks." She was still sweating because she had walked all the way from the car. It spoiled her powder. She sparkled her rings and dabbed at her face.

"Three lumps," she said. "And I'm sure Jack will be very happy here."

"Happy as sandboys." Gwilym sat down.

"Now, you must have some peaches, Mrs. Williams, they're lovely."

"They should be, they've been here long enough," said Gwilym.

Annie rattled the tea-cups at him again.

"No peaches, thanks," Mrs. Williams said.

"Oh, you must, Mrs. Williams, just one. With cream."

"No, no, Mrs. Jones, thanks the same," she said. "I don't mind pears or chunks, but I can't bear peaches."

Jack and I had stopped talking. Annie stared down at her gym shoes. One of the two clocks on the mantelpiece coughed, and struck. Mrs. Williams struggled from her chair.

"There, time flies!" she said.

She pushed her way past the furniture, jostled against the cupboard, rattled the trinkets and brooches, and kissed Jack on the forehead.

"You've got scent on," he said.

She patted my head.

"Now, behave yourselves."

To Annie, she said in a whisper: "And remember, Mrs. Jones, just good plain food. No spoiling his appetite."

Annie followed her out of the room. She moved slowly now. "I'll do my very best, Mrs. Williams."

We heard her say, "Good-bye then, Mrs. Williams," and go down the steps of the kitchen and close the door. The motorcar roared in the yard, then the noise grew softer and died.

Down the thick dingle Jack and I ran shouting, scalping the brambles with our thin stick-hatchets, dancing, hallooing. We skidded to a stop and prowled on the busy banks of the stream. Up above, sat one-eyed, dead-eyed, sinister, slim, tennotched Gwilym, loading his guns in Gallows Farm. We crawled and rat-tatted through the bushes, hid, at a whistled signal, in the deep grass, and crouched there, waiting for the crack of a twig or the secret breaking of boughs.

On my haunches, eager and alone, casting an ebony shadow, with the Gorsehill jungle swarming, the violent, impossible birds and fishes leaping, hidden under four-stemmed flowers the height of horses, in the early evening in a dingle near Carmarthen, my friend Jack Williams invisibly near me, I felt all my young body like an excited animal surrounding me, the torn knees bent, the bumping heart, the long heat and depth between the legs, the sweat prickling in the hands, the tunnels down to the ear-drums, the little balls of dirt between the toes, the eyes in the sockets, the tucked-up voice, the blood racing, the memory around and within flying, jumping, swimming, and waiting to pounce. There, playing Indians in the evening, I was aware of me myself in the exact middle of a living story, and my body was my adventure and my name. I sprang with excitement and scrambled up through the scratching brambles again.

Jack cried: "I see you! I see you!" He scampered after me. "Bang! bang! you're dead!"

But I was young and loud and alive, though I lay down obediently.

"Now you try and kill me," said Jack. "Count a hundred."

I closed one eye, saw him rush and stamp towards the upper field, then tiptoe back and begin to climb a tree, and I counted fifty and ran to the foot of the tree and killed him as he climbed. "You fall down," I said.

He refused to fall, so I climbed too, and we clung to the top branches and stared down at the lavatory in the corner of the field. Gwilym was sitting on the seat with his trousers down. He looked small and black. He was reading a book and moving his hands.

"We can see you!" we shouted.

He snatched his trousers up and put the book in his pocket.

"We can see you, Gwilym!"

He came out into the field. "Where are you, then?"

We waved our caps at him.

"In the sky!" Jack shouted.

"Flying!" I shouted.

We stretched our arms out like wings.

"Fly down here."

We swung and laughed on the branches.

"There's birds!" cried Gwilym.

Our jackets were torn and our stockings were wet and our shoes were sticky; we had green moss and brown bark on our hands and faces when we went in for supper and a scolding. Annie was quiet that night, though she called me a ragamuffin and said she didn't know what Mrs. Williams would think and told Gwilym he should know better. We made faces at Gwilym and put salt in his tea, but after supper he said: "You can come to chapel if you like. Just before bed."

He lit a candle on the top of the pulpit cart. It was a small light in the big barn. The bats were gone. Shadows still clung upside down along the roof. Gwilym was no longer my cousin in a Sunday suit, but a tall stranger shaped like a spade in a cloak, and his voice grew too deep. The straw heaps were lively. I thought of the sermon on the cart: we were watched, Jack's heart was watched, Gwilym's tongue was marked down, my whisper, "Look at the little eyes," was remembered always.

"Now I take confessions," said Gwilym from the cart.

Jack and I stood bareheaded in the circle of the candle, and I could feel the trembling of Jack's body.

"You first." Gwilym's finger, as bright as though he had held it in the candle flame until it burned, pointed me out, and I took a step towards the pulpit cart, raising my head.

"Now you confess," said Gwilym.

"What have I got to confess?"

"The worst thing you've done."

I let Edgar Reynolds be whipped because I had taken his homework; I stole from my mother's bag; I stole from Gwyneth's bag; I stole twelve books in three visits from the library, and threw them away in the park; I beat a dog with a stick so that it would roll over and lick my hand afterwards; I cut my knee with a pen-knife, and put the blood on my handkerchief and said it had come out of my ears so that I could pretend I was ill and frighten my mother; I saw Billy Jones beat a pigeon to death with a fire-shovel, and laughed and got sick; Cedric Williams and I broke into Mrs. Samuels's house and poured ink over the bedclothes.

I said: "I haven't done anything bad."

"Go on, confess!" said Gwilym. He was frowning down at me.

"I can't! I can't!" I said. "I haven't done anything bad."

"Go on, confess!"

"I won't! I won't!"

Jack began to cry. "I want to go home," he said.

Gwilym opened the chapel door and we followed him into the yard, down past the black, humped sheds, towards the house, and Jack sobbed all the way.

In bed together, Jack and I confessed our sins.

"I steal from my mother's bag, too; there are pounds and pounds."

"How much do you steal?"

"Threepence."

"I killed a man once."

"No you didn't then."

"Honest to Christ, I shot him through the heart."

"What was his name?"

"Williams."

"Did he bleed?"

I thought the stream was lapping against the side of the house.

"Like a bloody pig," I said.

Jack's tears had dried. "I don't like Gwilym, he's barmy."

"No, he isn't. I found a lot of poems in his bedroom once. They were all written to girls. And he showed them to me afterwards, and he'd changed all the girls' names to God."

"He's religious."

"No he isn't, he goes with actresses. He knows Corinne Griffiths."

Our door was open. I liked the door locked at night, because I would rather have a ghost in the bedroom than think of one coming in; but Jack liked it open, and we tossed and he won. We heard the front door rattle and footsteps in the kitchen passage.

"That's Uncle Jim."

"What's he like?"

"He's like a fox, he eats pigs and chickens."

The ceiling was thin and we heard every sound, the creaking of the bard's chair, the clatter of plates, Annie's voice saying: "Midnight!"

"He's drunk," I said. We lay quite still, hoping to hear a quarrel.

"Perhaps he'll throw plates," I said.

But Annie scolded him softly: "There's a fine state, Jim." He murmured to her.

"There's one pig gone," she said. "Oh, why do you have to do it, Jim? There's nothing left now. We'll never be able to carry on."

"Money! money! money!" he said. I knew he would be lighting his pipe.

Then Annie's voice grew so soft we could not hear the words, and uncle said: "Did she pay you the thirty shillings?"

"They're talking about your mother," I told Jack.

For a long time Annie spoke in a low voice, and we waited for words. "Mrs. Williams", she said, and "motor-car", and "Jack", and "peaches". I thought she was crying, for her voice broke on the last word.

Uncle Jim's chair creaked again, he might have struck his fist on the table, and we heard him shout: "I'll give her peaches! Peaches, peaches! Who does she think she is? Aren't peaches good enough for her? To hell with her bloody motor-car and her bloody son! Making us small."

"Don't, don't, Jim!" Annie said. "You'll wake the boys."

"I'll wake them and whip the hell out of them, too!"

"Please, please, Jim!"

"You send the boy away," he said, "or I'll do it myself. Back to his three bloody houses."

Jack pulled the bedclothes over his head and sobbed into the pillow: "I don't want to hear, I don't want to hear. I'll write to my mother. She'll take me away."

I climbed out to close the door. Jack would not talk to me again, and I fell asleep to the noise of the voices below, which soon grew gentle.

Uncle Jim was not at breakfast. When we came down, Jack's shoes were cleaned for him and his jacket was darned and pressed. Annie gave two boiled eggs to Jack and one to me. She forgave me when I drank tea from the saucer.

After breakfast, Jack walked to the post office. I took the one-eyed collie to chase rabbits in the upper fields, but it barked at ducks and brought me a tramp's shoe from a hedge, and lay down with its tail wagging in a rabbit hole. I threw stones at the deserted duck pond, and the collie ambled back with sticks.

Jack went skulking into the damp dingle, his hands in his pockets, his cap over one eye. I left the collie sniffing at a molehill, and climbed to the tree-top in the corner of the lavatory field. Below me, Jack was playing Indians all alone, scalping through the bushes, surprising himself round a tree, hiding from himself in the grass. I called to him once, but he pretended not to hear. He played alone, silently and savagely. I saw him standing with his hands in his pockets, swaying like a Kelly, on the mud-bank by the stream at the foot of the dingle. My bough lurched, the heads of the dingle bushes spun up towards me like green tops, "I'm falling!" I cried, my trousers saved me, I swung and grasped, this was one minute of wild adventure, but Jack did not look up and the minute was lost. I climbed, without dignity, to the ground.

Early in the afternoon, after a silent meal, when Gwilym was reading the scriptures or writing hymns to girls or sleeping in his chapel, Annie was baking bread, and I was cutting a wooden whistle in the loft over the stable, the motor-car drove up in the yard again.

Out of the house Jack, in his best suit, ran to meet his mother, and I heard him say as she stepped, raising her short skirts, on to the cobbles: "And he called you a bloody cow, and he said he'd whip the hell out of me, and Gwilym took me to the barn in the dark and let the mice run over me, and Dylan's a thief, and that old woman's spoilt my jacket."

Mrs. Williams sent the chauffeur for Jack's luggage. Annie came to the door, trying to smile and curtsy, tidying her hair, wiping her hands on her pinafore.

Mrs. Williams said, "Good afternoon," and sat with Jack in the back of the car and stared at the ruin of Gorsehill.

The chauffeur came back. The car drove off, scattering the hens. I ran out of the stable to wave to Jack. He sat still and stiff by his mother's side. I waved my handkerchief.

The ending was a sad one, for the boy. How sad is the author, in telling us about it? Why is there this difference?

Jack is not an unpleasant boy, is he? Imagine the story as he would tell it, thinking of his point of view.

Notice Thomas's particular handling of words, which is unusual and can teach us a good deal. The verbs and adjectives are simple, but strong and concrete—look at the description of the farmyard on page 16, or of the boy's excited awareness, on page 23, of "me myself in the exact middle of a living story".

This is clear and easily involves the reader.

Be alert to the casually mentioned details, many of which are little jokes in themselves. For example, the light shining in the supposedly deserted house where Uncle Jim says a hangman lived; or Mrs. Williams on page 20 compared to a ship; or the clock on page 22 which "coughed, and struck".

Occasionally the writer's mischievous enjoyment of words almost runs away with him and may strike you as a little over-done. How much this matters, you must decide. THE PEACHES *is, I think, an immensely entertaining story; nor is it lacking in human sympathy and vitality. Re-read it when you have read most of the stories in this book; and see if you then feel inclined to modify your first opinion.*

FOR FURTHER READING: Several other stories in *Portrait of the Artist as a Young Dog*. The *Collected Poems 1934–1952*; in particular, after this story, the poems *Fern Hill* and *In Memory of Ann Jones*—though the latter is very tricky.

GEOFFREY DUTTON

Geoffrey Dutton is an Australian, and this story captures a region and a situation which most British readers will never experience in "real life". Yet we can gain exciting and valuable experience from fiction, if it is well written; and the precision and vividness of this story make it disturbingly real.

The Wedge-Tailed Eagle

Through the hot, cloudless days in the back of New South Wales, there is always something beside the sun watching you from the sky. Over the line of the hills, or above the long stretches of plains, a black dot swings round and round; and its circles rise slowly or fall slowly, or simply remain at the same height, swinging in endless indolent curves, while the eyes watch the miles of earth below, and the six- or maybe nine-foot wingspan remains motionless in the air. You know that there is nothing you can do which will not be observed, that the circling eagle, however small the distance may make it, however aloof its flight may seem, has always fixed upon the earth an attention as fierce as its claws.

But the eagles watch the sky as well as the earth, and not only for other birds; when an Air Force station was established in their country in 1941, they were not alarmed by the noisy yellow aeroplanes. Occasionally they would even float in circles across the aerodrome itself, and then disappear again behind the hills; the pilots had little fear of colliding with one of these circling, watchful birds. The vast, brown-black shape of the eagle would appear before the little Tiger Moth biplane and then be gone. There was nothing more to it. No question of haste or flapping of wings, simply a flick over and down and then the eagle would resume its circling. Sometimes a pilot would chase the bird and would find, unexpectedly, no response; the eagle would seem not to notice the aeroplane and hold the course of its circling until the very moment when collision seemed inevitable. Then there would be the quick turn over, under, or away from the plane, with the great span of the wings unstirred. The delay and the quick manœuvre would be done with a princely detachment and consciousness of superiority, the eagle in the silence of its wings scorning the roar and fuss of the aircraft and its engine.

Two pilots from the station were drinking one day in the local town with one of the farmers over whose land they used to fly.

"Two of us, you know, could do it," one of them said. "By yourself it's hopeless. The eagle can outfly you without moving his wings. But with two of you, one could chase him round while the other climbed above and dived at him. That way you'd at last get him flustered."

The farmer was not at all hopeful.

"Maybe it'd take more than a couple of planes to fluster an eaglehawk. There's a big one around my place, just about twelve feet across. I wish you could get him. Though if you did hit him, there mightn't be much left of your little aeroplane."

"It always beats me why you call them eaglehawks," said one of the pilots. "The wedge-tailed eagle is the biggest eagle in the world. You ought to pay him more respect, the most magnificent, majestic bird there is."

The farmer was hostile to this idea of majesty.

"Have you ever seen them close-up? Or ever seen them feeding? The king of birds landing on a lolly-legged lamb and tearing him to bits. Or an old, dead, fly-blown ewe that's been fool enough to lie down with her legs uphill. Watch him hacking his way into their guts, with the vermin dancing all over his stinking brown feathers. Then all you've got to do is to let him see you five hundred yards off and up he flaps, slow and awkward, to a myall where he sits all bunched-up looking as if he's going to overbalance the little tree. Still, go ahead with your scheme. I'd like to see you beat one at his own game."

He left, and the two others continued discussing their plans. A pilot in a small, aerobatic aircraft is like a child. He longs for something to play with. He can be happy enough, rolling and looping by himself in the sky, but happiness changes to a kind of ecstasy when there is someone against whom to match his skill, or someone to applaud him when he low-flies through the unforeseeable complications of tree and rock, hill and river. The contest becomes more wonderful the nearer it approaches death, when all else is forgotten in the concentration of the minute. The pilot who fights with bullets and shells is ecstatically involved in his action. This fight with the wedge-tailed eagle was to be to the death, not a battle of bullets or shells, but of skill against inborn mastery. The risk of death would be there, just the same, both for the bird and for the pilot supported by the fragile wood and fabric of the aeroplane.

One cloudless morning the pilots flew off together, in close formation, towards the valley of the farmer's house. The sky was as clean as a gun-barrel and the sun hit them both in the back of the neck as they flew westward towards the scrubby range and the valley beyond. The pilot of the leading aircraft loosened his helmet and let the wind, like a cool rushing sense of elation and freedom, blow around his neck and hair. Like the eagle, he was a watcher, one from whom no secrets could hide on the earth below. The country matched the element in which he moved: both hard and unforgiving of mistakes, yet endlessly stretching, magnificent in freedom. Neither the air nor this land would bring anything for the asking; but they would offer all manner of their peculiar riches to anyone who could conquer them by work and vigilance and love. The foolish and the weak perished like the sheep stuck in the wet mud of the drying dams, in sight of the water for the lack of which they died.

As he approached the hills, the earth below him and the creeks were brown and dry as a walnut, with a strip of green along the river and a few bright squares where a farmer had sunk a bore and put in a few acres of lucerne. A mob of sheep stirred along in a cloud of dust through a few scattered myalls and gum trees. He finally bounced over the hills through air rough from the hot rocks, and turning away from the other aeroplane, moved up the broad valley, searching the sky for the black dot of an eagle wheeling and wheeling like a windmill on its side. There was no sign of anything, not even of a cloud or a high whirly of dust, which in an empty sky looks like a patch of rust in a gun-barrel. Everything seemed to him shiny and empty, yet somehow waiting to go off.

He made a long leisurely run up the valley, a few feet above the ground, lifting his wing over a fence or two, turning round a gum tree or away from a mob of sheep. The only other sign of life was the farmer standing near his truck by the gate of a paddock. He answered his wave, turned and flew over him, and then continued up the valley. Above him, in the other aeroplane, his friend waited for something to happen.

He ran his wheels almost along the ground and turned another fence. Suddenly the whole top of a tree flapped off in front of him and the eagle disappeared behind him before he

33

could turn. Another bird rose from a dead sheep a few hundred yards away, but the pilot's whole attention was concentrated on the bird that had risen from the myall tree. It was undoubtedly the big eagle of which the farmer had told them.

By the time he had turned and come back in a climb the eagle was five hundred feet above him. He opened the throttle wide and pulled the strap of his helmet tight. He looked for the other plane and saw that his friend was moving towards them and climbing also, so that with the added height he could dive as they had planned.

The pilot was astonished to find that he was being outclimbed without the bird even moving a feather of its wings. On the hot, unseen currents it swung lazily round and round, its motionless wings always above the quivering, roaring aircraft. To make things worse, the pilot, in order to climb as quickly as possible, had to move in a straight line and then turn back, whereas the eagle sailed up in a close spiral. His hand pushed harder on the small knob of the throttle already wide open against the stop. Perhaps the battle would come to no more than this, the noisy pursuit of an enemy who could never be reached.

Yet the eagle, its mastery already established, now deliberately ceased climbing and waited for the aeroplane to struggle up to its level. The pilot, wondering if the farmer below had seen his humiliation, pressed on above the bird, where at about three thousand feet he levelled off and waved to his friend above that the battle was about to begin.

He came round in a curve at the bird, the aeroplane on the edge of stalling, juddering all over, the control-stick suddenly going limp in his hand as a pump-handle when a tank is dry, the slots on the end of the wings clattering above him; and then, just as he ducked his head to avoid the shining curved beak, the braced black and brown feathers, the sky amazingly was empty in front of him. The eagle had flicked over as lightly as a swallow, with no sign of panic or haste. He looked over and saw it below him, circling as quietly as if nothing in the whole morning, in the sky or on the land, had disturbed its watchful mastery of the air.

As the pilot dived towards it and followed it around again, he saw his friend drop his wing and come down, steep and straight, to make the attack they had planned. He could see that the eagle, under its apparent negligence, was watching him and not the diving plane. This was the moment for which they had waited, when the eagle would break away as usual, but to find another aeroplane coming at it before it had time to move. The pilot's heart lunged inside him like the needle of the revolution counter on the instrument panel. Waiting until his friend had only another few hundred feet of his dive left, he jerked the controls hard over towards the shining feathers of the bird. It turned and fell below him, exactly as they had hoped it would. The pilot pulled himself up against his straps to watch its flight. The other aeroplane was on it just as it began its circling again. But the collision did not happen. The plane shot on and began to pull up out of its dive; the eagle recovered again into its slow swinging, a few hundred feet lower.

Yet it had shown a little concern. For the first time a fraction of dignity had been lost: momentarily the great wings had been disturbed a little from their full stretch. It had been startled into a quick defensive action. The pilot's excitement now blotted out everything but the battle in progress, leaving him poised between earth and sky, forgetful of both except as a blur of blue, a rush of brown. The last thing he saw on land had been the farmer's truck coming across the paddocks to a point somewhere below. Then all the vanity and pride in him had responded to the fact that there was someone to watch him. Now no response existed except to the detail of the black, polished brownness of the eagle's plumage, the glistening beak, the wedge-shaped tail. His excitement was at that intensity which is part of hope, his first sight of achievement. Previously the insolent negligence of the bird had destroyed his confidence, and had almost made the air feel the alien element it really was. In contrast with all his noisy manœuvring, his juggling with engine and controls, the eagle had scorned him with its silence, with its refusal to flap its wings, its mastery of the motionless sweep, the quick flick to safety and then the motionless circling again. The pilot had begun to wonder who was playing with whom. Perhaps the bird would suddenly turn, dive, rip him with a talon, and slide sideways down the vast slope to earth.

Yet now the eagle had been forced to move its wings, and he had seen the first sign of victory. Sweat poured round his helmet and down his neck and chest. His shirt clung wetly first to his flesh and then to the parachute harness. He looked at his altimeter and saw that they were down to seven hundred feet. Above him his friend was ready.

He turned in again towards the eagle. The aeroplane shivered and clung to height, on the last fraction of speed before the spin. Feeling the stiffness of his hands and feet on the controls, he told himself to relax like the eagle in front of him. He looked quickly upwards and saw his friend begin to dive. This was the second stage of their plan. The eagle, however little sign of it appeared, knew now that both aeroplanes were attacking. It circled, still on unmoving wings, but subtler and harder to follow, and shifted height slightly as it swung around.

The other plane was almost past him in its dive when he completed his turn in a vicious swing towards the eagle; he missed, spun, corrected, looked up to see the other aeroplane, which had dived this time far below the eagle, coming almost vertically up below the just-levelled bird.

The eagle heard and saw, and flicked over to where, before, safety had always been emptily waiting for it. It flashed, wings still gloriously outstretched, straight into the right-hand end of the upper mainplane of the aircraft, exactly where the metal slot curves across the wood and fabric. Its right wing, at the point where the hard, long feathers give way to the soft, curved feathers of the body, snapped away and fluttered down to earth. The left wing folded into the body, stretched and folded again, as the heavy box of bone, beak and claw plunged and slewed to the ground. The pilot could not watch the last few feet of its descent. For the first time he was grateful to the roar of the motor that obscured the thud of the body striking earth.

The two pilots landed in the paddock, and, leaving the engines running, walked over to the dark mass of feathers. One of them turned off to the side and came back holding the severed wing. It was almost as big as the man himself.

The two of them stood in silence. The moment of skill and danger was past, and the dead body before them proclaimed their victory. Frowning with the glare of the sun and the misery of their achievement they both looked down at the piteous, one-winged eagle. Not a mark of blood was on it, the beak glistening and uncrushed, the ribbed feet and talons clenched together. It was not the fact of death that kept them in silence; the watcher could not always keep his station in the air. What both of them could still see was the one-winged heap of bone and feathers, slewing and jerking uncontrolled to earth.

In the distance they heard the noise of the farmer's truck approaching, and saw it stop at a gate and the farmer wave as he got out to open it. They quickly picked up the bird and its wing, and ran with them to the little hillock covered in rocks at the corner of the paddock. Between two large rocks they folded both wings across the bird and piled stones above it;

and then, each lifting, carried a large flat stone and placed it above the others.

As they ran back towards the aeroplane a black dot broke from the hills and swung out above them, circling round and round, watching the truck accelerate and then stop as the two aeroplanes turned, taxied and slid into the air before it could reach them.

"The moment of skill and danger was past, the dead body before them proclaimed their victory." How much of a victory?

What is the value of the farmer's speech against the eagles, early on? If the pilots are right about the "majesty" of the birds, is the farmer wrong, in what he says?

Why, at the end, do the pilots hurry off when they see the farmer coming? And why do they first bury the eagle?

Some people would say this was not a "proper" short story, because it has no "twist" (or has it?). Such distinctions seem to me off the point; what matters is how good *the whatever-we-call-it is. This, I think, is very good; but in several ways it is like a poem rather than the other stories in this book. Notice, for example, how the comparisons which occur are in keeping with the story's setting, and support it instead of distracting: "brown and dry as a walnut"; "limp . . . as a pump-handle when a tank is dry"; "like the needle . . . on the instrument panel"; and the repeated likening of the sky to a gun-barrel—"shiny and empty, yet somehow waiting to go off". This care of suggestion, though excellent in fiction, is particularly the characteristic of poetry.*

Also, beneath the keen physical detail is a fierce emotional excitement. Notice how many large abstractions are introduced —"mastery", "freedom", "vanity", "pride", "the fact of death". Is this overloading the writing, or are such things really implied in the story of the men and the eagle?

38

KATHERINE MANSFIELD

Katherine Mansfield was born in New Zealand, where this story is set, but spent her adulthood in Europe. During her short life (1888–1923) she specialized in the short story, mastering the art of quick sensitive sketching of an emotion or a scene, usually, as in *Her First Ball*, from a girl's point of view. Although the ball in this story is at the turn of the century, and customs have changed considerably, it is a modern story, in its freedom of movement (a sort of darting along in time with Leila's perceptions) and in its swift, teasing mixture of moods.

Her First Ball

Exactly when the ball began Leila would have found it hard to say. Perhaps her first real partner was the cab. It did not matter that she shared the cab with the Sheridan girls and their brother. She sat back in her own little corner of it, and the bolster on which her hand rested felt like the sleeve of an unknown young man's suit; and away they bowled, past waltzing lamp-posts and houses and fences and trees.

"Have you really never been to a ball before, Leila? But, my child, how too weird——" cried the Sheridan girls.

39

"Our nearest neighbour was fifteen miles," said Leila softly, gently opening and shutting her fan.

Oh, dear, how hard it was to be indifferent like the others! She tried not to smile too much; she tried not to care. But every single thing was so new and exciting . . . Meg's tuberoses, Jose's long loop of amber, Laura's little dark head, pushing above her white fur like a flower through snow. She would remember for ever. It even gave her a pang to see her cousin Laurie throw away the wisps of tissue paper he pulled from the fastenings of his new gloves. She would like to have kept those wisps as a keepsake, as a remembrance. Laurie leaned forward and put his hand on Laura's knee.

"Look here, darling," he said. "The third and the ninth as usual. Twig?"

Oh, how marvellous to have a brother! In her excitement Leila felt that if there had been time, if it hadn't been impossible, she couldn't have helped crying because she was an only child and no brother had ever said "Twig?" to her; no sister would ever say, as Meg said to Jose that moment, "I've never known your hair go up more successfully than it has tonight!"

But, of course, there was no time. They were at the drill hall already; there were cabs in front of them and cabs behind. The road was bright on either side with moving fan-like lights, and on the pavement gay couples seemed to float through the air; little satin shoes chased each other like birds.

"Hold on to me, Leila; you'll get lost," said Laura.

"Come on, girls, let's make a dash for it," said Laurie.

Leila put two fingers on Laura's pink velvet cloak, and they were somehow lifted past the big golden lantern, carried along the passage, and pushed into the little room marked "Ladies". Here the crowd was so great there was hardly space to take off their things; the noise was deafening. Two benches on either side were stacked high with wraps. Two old women in white aprons ran up and down tossing fresh armfuls. And everybody was pressing forward trying to get at the little dressing-table and mirror at the far end.

A great quivering jet of gas lighted the ladies' room. It couldn't wait; it was dancing already. When the door opened again and there came a burst of tuning from the drill hall, it leaped almost to the ceiling.

Dark girls, fair girls were patting their hair, tying ribbons again, tucking handkerchiefs down the fronts of their bodices, smoothing marble-white gloves. And because they were all laughing it seemed to Leila that they were all lovely.

"Aren't there any invisible hairpins?" cried a voice. "How most extraordinary! I can't see a single invisible hairpin."

"Powder my back, there's a darling," cried someone else.

"But I must have a needle and cotton. I've torn simply miles and miles of the frill," wailed a third.

Then, "Pass them along, pass them along!" The straw basket of programmes was tossed from arm to arm. Darling little pink-and-silver programmes, with pink pencils and fluffy tassels. Leila's fingers shook as she took one out of the basket. She wanted to ask someone, "Am I meant to have one too?" but she had just time to read: "Waltz 3. *Two, Two in a Canoe*. Polka 4. *Making the Feathers Fly*," when Meg cried, "Ready, Leila?" and they pressed their way through the crush in the passage towards the big double doors of the drill hall.

Dancing had not begun yet, but the band had stopped tuning, and the noise was so great it seemed that when it did begin to play it would never be heard. Leila, pressing close to Meg, looking over Meg's shoulder, felt that even the little quivering coloured flags strung across the ceiling were talking. She quite forgot to be shy; she forgot how in the middle of dressing she had sat down on the bed with one shoe off and one shoe on and begged her mother to ring up her cousins and say she couldn't go after all. And the rush of longing she had

had to be sitting on the veranda of their forsaken up-country home, listening to the baby owls crying "More pork" in the moonlight, was changed to a rush of joy so sweet that it was hard to bear alone. She clutched her fan, and, gazing at the gleaming, golden floor, the azaleas, the lanterns, the stage at one end with its red carpet and gilt chairs and the band in one corner, she thought breathlessly, "How heavenly; how simply heavenly!"

All the girls stood grouped together at one side of the doors, the men at the other, and the chaperones in dark dresses, smiling rather foolishly, walked with little careful steps over the polished floor towards the stage.

"This is my little country cousin Leila. Be nice to her. Find her partners; she's under my wing," said Meg, going up to one girl after another.

Strange faces smiled at Leila—sweetly, vaguely. Strange voices answered, "Of course, my dear." But Leila felt the girls didn't really see her. They were looking towards the men. Why didn't the men begin? What were they waiting for? There they stood, smoothing their gloves, patting their glossy hair and smiling among themselves. Then, quite suddenly, as if they had only just made up their minds that that was what they had to do, the men came gliding over the parquet. There was a joyful flutter among the girls. A tall, fair man flew up to Meg, seized her programme, scribbled something; Meg passed him on to Leila. "May I have the pleasure?" He ducked and smiled. There came a dark man wearing an eyeglass, then cousin Laurie with a friend, and Laura with a little freckled fellow whose tie was crooked. Then quite an old man—fat, with a big bald patch on his head—took her programme and murmured, "Let me see, let me see!" And he was a long time comparing his programme, which looked black with names, with hers. It seemed to give him so much trouble that Leila was ashamed. "Oh, please don't bother," she said eagerly. But instead of replying the fat man wrote something, glanced at her again. "Do I remember this bright little face?" he said softly. "Is it known to me of yore?" At that moment the band began playing; the fat man disappeared. He was tossed away on a great wave of music that came flying over the gleaming floor, breaking the groups up into couples, scattering them, sending them spinning. . . .

Leila had learnt to dance at boarding school. Every Saturday afternoon the boarders were hurried off to a little corrugated iron mission hall where Miss Eccles (of London) held her "select" classes. But the difference between the dusty-smelling hall—with calico texts on the walls, the poor, terrified little woman in a brown velvet toque with rabbit's ears thumping the cold piano, Miss Eccles poking the girls' feet with her long white wand—and this, was so tremendous that Leila was sure if her partner didn't come and she had to listen to that marvellous music and to watch the others sliding, gliding over the golden floor, she would die at least, or faint, or lift her arms and fly out of one of those dark windows that showed the stars.

"Ours, I think——" Someone bowed, smiled, and offered her his arm; she hadn't to die after all. Someone's hand pressed her waist, and she floated away like a flower that is tossed into a pool.

"Quite a good floor, isn't it?" drawled a faint voice close to her ear.

"I think it's most beautifully slippery," said Leila.

"Pardon!" The faint voice sounded surprised. Leila said it again. And there was a tiny pause before the voice echoed, "Oh, quite!" and she was swung round again.

He steered so beautifully. That was the great difference between dancing with girls and men, Leila decided. Girls banged into each other and stamped on each other's feet; the girl who was gentleman always clutched you so.

The azaleas were separate flowers no longer; they were pink and white flags streaming by.

"Were you at the Bells' last week?" the voice came again. It sounded tired. Leila wondered whether she ought to ask him if he would like to stop.

"No, this is my first dance," said she.

Her partner gave a little gasping laugh. "Oh, I say," he protested.

"Yes, it is really the first dance I've ever been to." Leila was most fervent. It was such a relief to be able to tell somebody. "You see, I've lived in the country all my life up till now. . . ."

At that moment the music stopped and they went to sit on two chairs against the wall. Leila tucked her pink satin feet under and fanned herself, while she blissfully watched the other couples passing and disappearing through the swing doors.

"Enjoying yourself, Leila?" asked Jose, nodding her golden head.

Laura passed and gave her the faintest little wink; it made Leila wonder for a moment whether she was quite grown up after all. Certainly her partner did not say very much. He coughed, tucked his handkerchief away, pulled down his waistcoat, took a minute thread off his sleeve. But it didn't matter. Almost immediately the band started and her second partner seemed to spring from the ceiling.

"Floor's not bad," said the new voice. Did one always begin with the floor? And then, "Were you at the Neaves' on Tuesday?" And again Leila explained. Perhaps it was a little strange that her partners were not more interested. For it was thrilling. Her first ball! She was only at the beginning of everything. It seemed to her that she had never known what the night was like before. Up till now it had been dark, silent, beautiful very often—oh yes—but mournful somehow. Solemn. And now it would never be like that again—it had opened dazzling bright.

"Care for an ice?" said her partner. And they went through the swing doors, down the passage, to the supper-room. Her cheeks burned, she was fearfully thirsty. How sweet the ices looked on little glass plates and how cold the frosted spoon was, iced too! And when they came back to the hall there was the fat man waiting for her by the door. It gave her quite a shock to see again how old he was; he ought to have been on the stage with the fathers and mothers. And when Leila compared him with her other partners he looked shabby. His waistcoat was creased, there was a button off his glove, his coat looked as if it was dusty with French chalk.

"Come along, little lady," said the fat man. He scarcely troubled to clasp her, and they moved away so gently, it was more like walking than dancing. But he had not said a word about the floor. "Your first dance, isn't it?" he murmured.

"How *did* you know?"

"Ah," said the fat man, "that's what it is to be old!" He wheezed faintly as he steered past an awkward couple. "You see, I've been doing this kind of thing for the last thirty years."

"Thirty years?" cried Leila. Twelve years before she was born!

"It hardly bears thinking about, does it?" said the fat man gloomily. Leila looked at his bald head, and she felt quite sorry for him.

"I think it's marvellous to be still going on," she said kindly.

"Kind little lady," said the fat man, and he pressed her a little closer and hummed a bar of the waltz. "Of course," he said, "you can't hope to last anything like as long as that. No-o," said the fat man, "long before that you'll be sitting up there on the stage, looking on, in your nice black velvet. And these pretty arms will have turned into little short fat ones, and you'll beat time with such a different kind of fan—a black ebony one." The fat man seemed to shudder. "And you'll smile away like the poor old dears up there, and point to your

45

daughter, and tell the elderly lady next to you how some dreadful man tried to kiss her at the club ball. And your heart will ache, ache"—the fat man squeezed her closer still, as if he really was sorry for that poor heart—"because no one wants to kiss you now. And you'll say how unpleasant these polished floors are to walk on, how dangerous they are. Eh, Mademoiselle Twinkletoes?" said the fat man softly.

Leila gave a light little laugh, but she did not feel like laughing. Was it—could it all be true? It sounded terribly true. Was this first ball only the beginning of her last ball, after all? At that the music seemed to change; it sounded sad, sad; it rose upon a great sigh. Oh, how quickly things changed! Why didn't happiness last for ever? For ever wasn't a bit too long.

"I want to stop," she said in a breathless voice. The fat man led her to the door.

"No," she said, "I won't go outside. I won't sit down. I'll just stand here, thank you." She leaned against the wall, tapping with her foot, pulling up her gloves and trying to smile. But deep inside her a little girl threw her pinafore over her head and sobbed. Why had he spoiled it all?

"I say, you know," said the fat man, "you mustn't take me seriously, little lady."

"As if I should!" said Leila, tossing her small dark head and sucking her underlip. . . .

Again the couples paraded. The swing doors opened and shut. Now new music was given out by the bandmaster. But Leila didn't want to dance any more. She wanted to be home, or sitting on the veranda listening to those baby owls. When she looked through the dark windows at the stars they had long beams like wings. . . .

But presently a soft, melting, ravishing tune began, and a young man with curly hair bowed before her. She would have to dance, out of politeness, until she could find Meg. Very

46

stiffly she walked into the middle; very haughtily she put her hand on his sleeve. But in one minute, in one turn, her feet glided, glided. The lights, the azaleas, the dresses, the pink faces, the velvet chairs, all became one beautiful flying wheel. And when her next partner bumped her into the fat man and he said, "Par*don*," she smiled at him more radiantly than ever. She didn't even recognize him again.

Leila is eighteen, at her first ball; the writer is a mature woman. Through whose eyes is the ball seen? If your answer is "Leila's", consider whether the greater wisdom of the writer isn't also implied all the time. How are the two points of view combined? Is there more, or less, of the writer's view here than in THE PEACHES?

The fat man, with his uncomfortable teasing, gives a seriousness to the story without which it might be too flimsy. What might be his reasons for speaking to Leila like this? Is it really so cruel? Does it ruin the ball for her? Or is it perhaps better for us and our happiness to know the truth of things, even if it is saddening?

This ball is described from the feminine side—quite a glimpse behind the scenes for a male reader! Imagine how this (or a modern dance; the customs may differ but the foundation is the same) might be described from a young man's point of view. Think especially of the details which would convey the atmosphere and the young man's feelings.

FOR FURTHER READING: Katherine Mansfield's *Collected Stories* (Constable).

ALAN PATON

Alan Paton became famous in 1948 with his first novel *Cry, the Beloved Country*; but his work for South Africa, where he was born in 1903 and where he has chosen to remain in spite of many risks, had begun much earlier and has continued unfalteringly ever since. As a novelist he has great power, but his first concern is for the improvement of race relations and the penal system in his country, and all his writing is directed to this end. For thirteen years he was Principal of a large boys' reformatory in Johannesburg, and it is clearly from this experience that *Ha'penny* is told.

Ha'penny

Of the six hundred boys at the reformatory, about one hundred were from ten to fourteen years of age. My Department had from time to time expressed the intention of taking them away, and of establishing a special institution for them, more like an industrial school than a reformatory. This would have been a good thing, for their offences were very trivial, and they would have been better by themselves. Had such a school been established, I should have liked to be Principal of it myself, for it would have been an easier job; small boys turn instinctively towards affection, and one controls them by it, naturally and easily.

Some of them, if I came near them, either on parade or in school or at football, would observe me watchfully, not directly or fully, but obliquely and secretly; sometimes I would surprise them at it, and make some small sign of recognition, which would satisfy them so that they would cease to observe me, and would give their full attention to the event of the moment. But I knew that my authority was thus confirmed and strengthened.

The secret relations with them were a source of continuous pleasure to me. Had they been my own children I would no doubt have given a greater expression to it. But often I would move through the silent and orderly parade, and stand by one of them. He would look straight in front of him with a little frown of concentration that expressed both childish awareness and manly indifference to my nearness. Sometimes I would tweak his ear, and he would give me a brief smile of acknowledgement, or frown with still greater concentration. It was natural, I suppose, to confine these outward expressions to the very smallest, but they were taken as symbolic, and some older boys would observe them and take themselves to be included. It was a relief, when the reformatory was passing through times of turbulence and trouble, and when there was danger of estrangement between authority and boys, to make those simple and natural gestures, which were reassurances to both me and them that nothing important had changed.

On Sunday afternoons when I was on duty I would take my car to the reformatory and watch the free boys being signed out at the gate. This simple operation was watched by many boys not free, who would tell each other, "In so many weeks I'll be signed out myself." Among the watchers were always some of the small boys, and these I would take by turns in the car. We would go out to the Potchefstroom Road with its ceaseless stream of traffic, and to the Baragwanath cross-roads, and come back by the Van Wyksrus road to the reformatory. I would talk to them about their families, their parents, their sisters and brothers, and I would pretend to know nothing of Durban, Port Elizabeth, Potchefstroom, and Clocolan, and ask them if these places were bigger than Johannesburg.

One of the small boys was Ha'penny, and he was about twelve years old. He came from Bloemfontein and was the biggest talker of them all. His mother worked in a white person's house, and he had two brothers and two sisters. His brothers were Richard and Dickie, and his sisters Anna and Mina.

"Richard and Dickie?" I asked.

"Yes, meneer."

"In English," I said, "Richard and Dickie are the same name."

When we returned to the reformatory, I sent for Ha'penny's papers; there it was plainly set down, Ha'penny was a waif, with no relatives at all. He had been taken in from one home to another, but he was naughty and uncontrollable, and eventually had taken to pilfering at the market.

I then sent for the Letter Book, and found that Ha'penny wrote regularly, or rather that others wrote for him till he could write himself, to Mrs. Betty Maarman, of 48 Vlak Street, Bloemfontein. But Mrs. Maarman had never once replied to him. When questioned, he had said, perhaps she is sick. I sat down and wrote at once to the Social Welfare Officer at Bloemfontein, asking him to investigate.

The next time I had Ha'penny out in the car I questioned him again about his family. And he told me the same as before, his mother, Richard and Dickie, Anna and Mina. But he softened the "D" of Dickie, so that it sounded now like Tickie.

"I thought you said Dickie," I said.

"I said Tickie," he said.

He watched me with concealed apprehension, and I came to the conclusion that this waif of Bloemfontein was a clever boy, who had told me a story that was all imagination, and had changed one single letter of it to make it safe from any question. And I thought I understood it all too, that he was ashamed of being without a family and had invented them all, so that no one might discover that he was fatherless and motherless and that no one in the world cared whether he was alive or dead. This gave me a strong feeling for him, and I went out of my way to manifest towards him that fatherly care that the State, though not in those words, had enjoined upon me by giving me this job.

Then the letter came from the Social Welfare Officer in Bloemfontein, saying that Mrs. Betty Maarman of 48 Vlak Street was a real person, and that she had four children, Richard and Dickie, Anna and Mina, but that Ha'penny was no child of hers, and she knew him only as a derelict of the streets. She had never answered his letters, because he wrote to her as "Mother", and she was no mother of his, nor did she wish to play any such role. She was a decent woman, a faithful member of the church, and she had no thought of corrupting her family by letting them have anything to do with such a child.

But Ha'penny seemed to me anything but the usual delinquent; his desire to have a family was so strong, and his reformatory record was so blameless, and his anxiety to please and obey so great, that I began to feel a great duty towards him. Therefore I asked him about his "mother".

He could not speak enough of her, nor with too high praise. She was loving, honest, and strict. Her home was clean. She had affection for all her children. It was clear that the homeless child, even as he had attached himself to me, would have attached himself to her; he had observed her even as he had observed me, but did not know the secret of how to open her heart, so that she would take him in, and save him from the lonely life that he led.

"Why did you steal when you had such a mother?" I asked.

He could not answer that; not all his brains nor his courage could find an answer to such a question, for he knew that with such a mother he would not have stolen at all.

"The boy's name is Dickie," I said, "not Tickie."

And then he knew the deception was revealed. Another boy might have said, "I told you it was Dickie," but he was too intelligent for that; he knew that if I had established that the boy's name was Dickie, I must have established other things too. I was shocked by the immediate and visible effect of my action. His whole brave assurance died within him, and he stood there exposed, not as a liar, but as a homeless child who had surrounded himself with mother, brothers, and sisters, who did not exist. I had shattered the very foundations of his pride, and his sense of human significance.

He fell sick at once, and the doctor said it was tuberculosis. I wrote at once to Mrs. Maarman, telling her the whole story, of how this small boy had observed her, and had decided that she was the person he desired for his mother. But she wrote back saying that she could take no responsibility for him. For one thing, Ha'penny was a Mosuto, and she was a coloured woman; for another, she had never had a child in trouble, and how could she take such a boy?

Tuberculosis is a strange thing; sometimes it manifests itself suddenly in the most unlikely host, and swiftly sweeps to the end. Ha'penny withdrew himself from the world, from all Principals and mothers, and the doctor said there was little hope. In desperation I sent money for Mrs. Maarman to come.

She was a decent, homely woman, and, seeing that the situation was serious, she, without fuss or embarrassment, adopted Ha'penny for her own. The whole reformatory accepted her as his mother. She sat the whole day with him, and talked to him of Richard and Dickie, Anna and Mina, and how they were all waiting for him to come home. She poured out her affection on him, and had no fear of his sickness, nor did she allow it to prevent her from satisfying his hunger to be owned. She talked to him of what they would do when he came back, and how he would go to the school, and what they would buy for Guy Fawkes night.

He in his turn gave his whole attention to her, and when I visited him he was grateful, but I had passed out of his world. I felt judged in that I had sensed only the existence and not the measure of his desire. I wished I had done something sooner, more wise, more prodigal.

We buried him on the reformatory farm, and Mrs. Maarman said to me, "When you put up the cross, put he was my son."

"I'm ashamed," she said, "that I wouldn't take him."

"The sickness," I said, "the sickness would have come."

"No," she said, shaking her head with certainty. "It wouldn't have come. And if it had come at home, it would have been different."

So she left for Bloemfontein, after her strange visit to a reformatory. And I was left too, with the resolve to be more prodigal in the task that the State, though not in so many words, had enjoined upon me.

This is very simple writing. Some other stories in this book use words in bold, extraordinary ways, to awaken a rich, even confused response on several levels; and that can be very exciting. But here Alan Paton doesn't want to confuse or bewitch us; the language is as clear and controlled as possible, to let the story speak for itself.

In South Africa a "coloured" person is someone of mixed blood, as distinct from "Africans", such as Ha'penny, as from "Europeans", such as the writer.

Make sure you understand what "prodigal" means. What lesson did the writer learn from these events?

FOR FURTHER READING: Alan Paton's novel *Cry, the Beloved Country* seems to me one of the greatest novels written since the Second World War. In telling a gripping and disturbing story about individual people it also presents the problems of South Africa today, and faces them with great intelligence and courage.

You will also enjoy the other stories in *Debbie Go Home,* from which *Ha'penny* is taken. Both books are published by Jonathan Cape.

TED HUGHES

Ted Hughes, a Yorkshireman born in 1930, has published very little fiction, but is one of the leading young poets in England today. His work has an original force which makes it easily distinguishable from that of any other poet I know. Much of his writing is about animals, and in so far as it has any forbear, resembles D. H. Lawrence's in its intense understanding of life in whatever form: both writers seem to enter, without strain, into the physical creature. This story, however, is at least as much about the man as about the horse; and it is deliberately rather puzzling.

The Rain Horse

As the young man came over the hill the first thin blowing of rain met him. He turned his coat-collar up and stood on top of the shelving rabbit-riddled hedgebank, looking down into the valley.

He had come too far. What had set out as a walk along pleasantly remembered tarmac lanes had turned dreamily by gate and path and hedge-gap into a cross-ploughland trek, his shoes ruined, the dark mud of the lower fields inching up the trouser legs of his grey suit where they rubbed against each other. And now there was a raw, flapping wetness in the air that would be downpour again at any minute. He shivered, holding himself tense against the cold.

This was the view he had been thinking of. Vaguely, without really directing his walk, he had felt he would get the whole thing from this point. For twelve years, whenever he had recalled this scene, he had imagined it as it looked from here. Now the valley, lay sunken in front of him, utterly deserted, shallow, bare fields, black and sodden as the bed of an ancient lake after the weeks of rain.

Nothing happened. Not that he had looked forward to any very transfiguring experience. But he had expected something, some pleasure, some meaningful sensation, he didn't quite know what.

So he waited, trying to nudge the right feelings alive with the details—the surprisingly familiar curve of the hedges, the stone gate-pillar and iron gatehook let into it that he had used as a target, the long bank of the rabbit-warren on which he stood and which had been the first thing he ever noticed about the hill when twenty years ago, from the distance of the village, he had said to himself "That looks like rabbits."

Twelve years had changed him. This land no longer recognized him, and he looked back at it coldly, as at a finally visited home-country, known only through the stories of a grandfather; felt nothing but the dullness of feeling nothing. Boredom. Then, suddenly, impatience, with a whole exasperated swarm of little anxieties about his shoes and the spitting rain and his new suit and that sky and the two-mile trudge through the mud back to the road.

It would be quicker to go straight forward to the farm a mile away in the valley and behind which the road looped. But the thought of meeting the farmer—to be embarrassingly remembered or shouted at as a trespasser—deterred him. He saw the rain pulling up out of the distance, dragging its grey broken columns, smudging the trees and the farms.

56

A wave of anger went over him: anger against himself for blundering into this mud-trap and anger against the land that made him feel so outcast, so old and stiff and stupid. He wanted nothing but to get away from it as quickly as possible. But as he turned, something moved in his eye-corner. All his senses startled alert. He stopped.

Over to his right a thin, black horse was running across the ploughland towards the hill, its head down, neck stretched out. It seemed to be running on its toes like a cat, like a dog up to no good.

From the high point on which he stood the hill dipped slightly and rose to another crested point fringed with the tops of trees, three hundred yards to his right. As he watched it, the horse ran up that crest, showed against the sky—for a moment like a nightmarish leopard—and disappeared over the other side.

For several seconds he stared at the skyline, stunned by the unpleasantly strange impression the horse had made on him. Then the plastering beat of icy rain on his bare skull brought him to himself. The distance had vanished in a wall of grey. All around him the fields were jumping and streaming.

Holding his collar close and tucking his chin down into it he ran back over the hilltop towards the town-side, the lee-side, his feet sucking and splashing, at every stride plunging to the ankle.

This hill was shaped like a wave, a gently rounded back lifting out of the valley to a sharply crested, almost concave front hanging over the river meadows towards the town. Down this front, from the crest, hung two small woods separated by a fallow field. The near wood was nothing more than a quarry, circular, full of stones and bracken, with a few thorns and nondescript saplings, foxholes and rabbit holes. The other was rectangular, mainly a planting of scrub oak trees. Beyond the river smouldered the town like a great heap of blue cinders.

He ran along the top of the first wood and finding no shelter but the thin, leafless thorns of the hedge, dipped below the crest out of the wind and jogged along through thick grass to the wood of oaks. In blinding rain he lunged through the barricade of brambles at the wood's edge. The little crippled trees were small choice in the way of shelter, but at a sudden fierce thickening of the rain he took one at random and crouched down under the leaning trunk.

Still panting from his run, drawing his knees up tightly, he watched the bleak lines of rain, grey as hail, slanting through the boughs into the clumps of bracken and bramble. He felt hidden and safe. The sound of the rain as it rushed and lulled in the wood seemed to seal him in. Soon the chilly sheet lead of his suit became a tight, warm mould, and gradually he sank into a state of comfort that was all but trance, though the rain beat steadily on his exposed shoulders and trickled down the oak trunk on to his neck.

All around him the boughs angled down, glistening, black as iron. From their tips and elbows the drops hurried steadily, and the channels of the bark pulsed and gleamed. For a time he amused himself calculating the variation in the rainfall by the variations in a dribble of water from a trembling twig-end two feet in front of his nose. He studied the twig, bringing dwarfs and continents and animals out of its scurfy bark. Beyond the boughs the blue shoal of the town was rising and falling, and darkening and fading again, in the pale, swaying backdrop of rain.

He wanted this rain to go on for ever. Whenever it seemed to be drawing off he listened anxiously until it closed in again. As long as it lasted he was suspended from life and time. He didn't want to return to his sodden shoes and his possibly ruined suit and the walk back over that land of mud.

All at once he shivered. He hugged his knees to squeeze out the cold and found himself thinking of the horse. The hair on the nape of his neck prickled slightly. He remembered how it had run up to the crest and showed against the sky.

He tried to dismiss the thought. Horses wander about the countryside often enough. But the image of the horse as it had appeared against the sky stuck in his mind. It must have come over the crest just above the wood in which he was now sitting. To clear his mind, he twisted around and looked up the wood between the tree stems, to his left.

At the wood top, with the silvered grey light coming in behind it, the black horse was standing under the oaks, its head high and alert, its ears pricked, watching him.

A horse sheltering from the rain generally goes into a sort of stupor, tilts a hind hoof and hangs its head and lets its eyelids droop, and so it stays as long as the rain lasts. This horse was nothing like that. It was watching him intently, standing perfectly still, its soaked neck and flank shining in the hard light.

He turned back. His scalp went icy and he shivered. What was he to do? Ridiculous to try driving it away. And to leave the wood, with the rain still coming down full pelt was out of the question. Meanwhile the idea of being watched became more and more unsettling until at last he had to twist around again, to see if the horse had moved. It stood exactly as before.

This was absurd. He took control of himself and turned back deliberately, determined not to give the horse one more thought. If it wanted to share the wood with him, let it. If it wanted to stare at him, let it. He was nestling firmly into these resolutions when the ground shook and he heard the crash of a heavy body coming down the wood. Like lightning his legs bounded him upright and about face. The horse was almost on top of him, its head stretching forward, ears flattened and lips lifted back from the long yellow teeth. He got one snap-shot glimpse of the red-veined eyeball as he flung himself backwards around the tree. Then he was away up the slope, whipped by oak twigs as he leapt the brambles and brush-wood, twisting between the close trees till he tripped and sprawled. As he fell the warning flashed through his head that he must at all costs keep his suit out of the leaf-mould, but a more urgent instinct was already rolling him violently side-ways. He spun around, sat up and looked back, ready to scramble off in a flash to one side. He was panting from the sudden excitement and effort. The horse had disappeared. The wood was empty except for the drumming, slant grey rain, dancing the bracken and glittering from the branches.

He got up, furious. Knocking the dirt and leaves from his suit as well as he could he looked around for a weapon. The horse was evidently mad, had an abscess on its brain or some-thing of the sort. Or maybe it was just spiteful. Rain some-times puts creatures into queer states. Whatever it was, he was going to get away from the wood as quickly as possible, rain or no rain.

Since the horse seemed to have gone on down the wood, his way to the farm over the hill was clear. As he went, he broke a yard length of wrist-thick dead branch from one of the oaks, but immediately threw it aside and wiped the slime of rotten wet bark from his hands with his soaked handkerchief. Al-ready he was thinking it incredible that the horse could have meant to attack him. Most likely it was just going down the wood for better shelter and had made a feint at him in passing —as much out of curiosity or playfulness as anything. He recalled the way horses menace each other when they are galloping round in a paddock.

The wood rose to a steep bank topped by the hawthorn hedge that ran along the whole ridge of the hill. He was pulling himself up to a thin place in the hedge by the bare stem of one of the hawthorns when he ducked and shrank down again. The swelling gradient of fields lay in front of him, smoking in the slowly crossing rain. Out in the middle of the first field, tall as a statue, and a ghostly silver in the under-cloud light, stood the horse, watching the wood.

He lowered his head slowly, slithered back down the bank and crouched. An awful feeling of helplessness came over him. He felt certain the horse had been looking straight at him. Waiting for him? Was it clairvoyant? Maybe a mad animal can be clairvoyant. At the same time he was ashamed to find himself acting so inanely, ducking and creeping about in this way just to keep out of sight of a horse. He tried to imagine how anybody in their senses would just walk off home. This cooled him a little, and he retreated farther down the wood. He would go back the way he had come, along under the hill crest, without any more nonsense.

The wood hummed and the rain was a cold weight, but he observed this rather than felt it. The water ran down inside his clothes and squelched in his shoes as he eased his way carefully over the bedded twigs and leaves. At every instant he expected to see the prick-eared black head looking down at him from the hedge above.

At the woodside he paused, close against a tree. The success of this last manœuvre was restoring his confidence, but he didn't want to venture out into the open field without making sure that the horse was just where he had left it. The perfect move would be to withdraw quietly and leave the horse standing out there in the rain. He crept up again among the trees to the crest and peered through the hedge.

The grey field and the whole slope were empty. He searched the distance. The horse was quite likely to have forgotten him altogether and wandered off. Then he raised himself and leaned out to see if it had come in close to the hedge. Before he was aware of anything the ground shook. He twisted around wildly to see how he had been caught. The black shape was above him, right across the light. Its whinnying snort and the spattering whack of its hooves seemed to be actually inside his head as he fell backwards down the bank, and leapt again like a madman, dodging among the oaks, imagining how the buffet would come and how he would be knocked headlong. Halfway down the wood the oaks gave way to bracken and old roots and stony rabbit diggings. He was well out into the middle of this before he realized that he was running alone.

Gasping for breath now and cursing mechanically, without a thought for his suit he sat down on the ground to rest his shaking legs, letting the rain plaster the hair down over his forehead and watching the dense flashing lines disappear abruptly into the soil all around him as if he were watching through thick plate glass. He took deep breaths in the effort to steady his heart and regain control of himself. His right trouser turn-up was ripped at the seam and his suit jacket was splashed with the yellow mud of the top field.

Obviously the horse had been farther along the hedge above the steep field, waiting for him to come out at the woodside just as he had intended. He must have peeped through the hedge—peeping the wrong way—within yards of it.

However, this last attack had cleared up one thing. He need no longer act like a fool out of mere uncertainty as to whether the horse was simply being playful or not. It was definitely after him. He picked two stones about the size of goose eggs and set off towards the bottom of the wood, striding carelessly.

A loop of the river bordered all this farmland. If he crossed the little level meadow at the bottom of the wood, he could follow the three-mile circuit, back to the road. There were deep hollows in the river-bank, shoaled with pebbles, as he remembered, perfect places to defend himself from if the horse followed him out there.

The hawthorns that choked the bottom of the wood—some of them good-sized trees—knitted into an almost impassable barrier. He had found a place where the growth thinned slightly and had begun to lift aside the long spiny stems, pushing himself forward, when he stopped. Through the bluish veil of bare twigs he saw the familiar shape out in the field below the wood.

But it seemed not to have noticed him yet. It was looking out across the field towards the river. Quietly, he released himself from the thorns and climbed back across the clearing towards the one side of the wood he had not yet tried. If the horse would only stay down there he could follow his first and easiest plan, up the wood and over the hilltop to the farm.

Now he noticed that the sky had grown much darker. The rain was heavier every second, pressing down as if the earth had to be flooded before nightfall. The oaks ahead blurred and the ground drummed. He began to run. And as he ran he heard a deeper sound running with him. He whirled around. The horse was in the middle of the clearing. It might have been running to get out of the terrific rain except that it was coming straight for him, scattering clay and stones, with an immensely supple and powerful motion. He let out a tearing roar and threw the stone in his right hand. The result was instantaneous. Whether at the roar or the stone the horse reared as if against a wall and shied to the left. As it dropped back on to its forefeet he flung his second stone, at ten yards' range, and saw a bright mud blotch suddenly appear on the glistening black flank. The horse surged down the wood, splashing the earth like water, tossing its long tail as it plunged out of sight among the hawthorns.

He looked around for stones. The encounter had set the blood beating in his head and given him a savage energy. He could have killed the horse at that moment. That this brute should pick him and play with him in this malevolent fashion was more than he could bear. Whoever owned it, he thought, deserved to have its neck broken for letting the dangerous thing loose.

He came out at the woodside, in open battle now, still

searching for the right stones. There were plenty here, piled and scattered where they had been ploughed out of the field. He selected two, then straightened and saw the horse twenty yards off in the middle of the steep field, watching him calmly. They looked at each other.

"Out of it!" he shouted, brandishing his arm. "Out of it! Go on!" The horse twitched its pricked ears. With all his force he threw. The stone soared and landed beyond with a soft thud. He re-armed and threw again. For several minutes he kept up his bombardment without a single hit, working himself up into a despair and throwing more and more wildly, till his arm began to ache with the unaccustomed exercise. Throughout the performance the horse watched him fixedly. Finally he had to stop and ease his shoulder muscles. As if the horse had been waiting for just this, it dipped its head twice and came at him.

He snatched up two stones and roaring with all his strength flung the one in his right hand. He was astonished at the crack of the impact. It was as if he had struck a tile—and the horse actually stumbled. With another roar he jumped forward and hurled his other stone. His aim seemed to be under superior guidance. The stone struck and rebounded straight up into the air, spinning fiercely, as the horse swirled away and went careering down towards the far bottom corner of the field, at first with great, swinging leaps, then at a canter, leaving deep churned holes in the soil.

It turned up the far side of the field, climbing till it was level with him. He felt a little surprise of pity to see it shaking its head, and once it paused to lower its head and paw over its ear with its forehoof as a cat does.

"You stay there!" he shouted. "Keep your distance and you'll not get hurt."

And indeed the horse did stop at that moment, almost obediently. It watched him as he climbed to the crest.

The rain swept into his face and he realized that he was freezing, as if his very flesh were sodden. The farm seemed miles away over the dreary fields. Without another glance at the horse—he felt too exhausted to care now what it did—he loaded the crook of his left arm with stones and plunged out on to the waste of mud.

He was half-way to the first hedge before the horse appeared, silhouetted against the sky at the corner of the wood, head high and attentive, watching his laborious retreat over the three fields.

The ankle-deep clay dragged at him. Every stride was a separate, deliberate effort, forcing him up and out of the sucking earth, burdened as he was by his sogged clothes and load of stones and limbs that seemed themselves to be turning to mud. He fought to keep his breathing even, two strides in, two strides out, the air ripping his lungs. In the middle of the last field he stopped and looked around. The horse, tiny on the skyline, had not moved.

At the corner of the field he unlocked his clasped arms and dumped the stones by the gatepost, then leaned on the gate. The farm was in front of him. He became conscious of the rain again and suddenly longed to stretch out full-length under it, to take the cooling, healing drops all over his body and forget himself in the last wretchedness of the mud. Making an effort, he heaved his weight over the gate-top. He leaned again, looking up at the hill.

Rain was dissolving land and sky together like a wet water-colour as the afternoon darkened. He concentrated, raising his head, searching the skyline from end to end. The horse had vanished. The hill looked lifeless and desolate, an island lifting out of the sea, awash with every tide.

Under the long shed where the tractors, plough, binders and the rest were drawn up, waiting for their seasons, he sat on a sack thrown over a petrol drum, trembling, his lungs heaving. The mingled smell of paraffin, creosote, fertilizer, dust—all was exactly as he had left it twelve years ago. The ragged swallows' nests were still there tucked in the angles of the rafters. He remembered three dead foxes hanging in a row from one of the beams, their teeth bloody.

The ordeal with the horse had already sunk from reality. It hung under the surface of his mind, an obscure confusion of fright and shame, as after a narrowly escaped street accident. There was a solid pain in his chest, like a spike of bone stabbing, that made him wonder if he had strained his heart on that last stupid burdened run. Piece by piece he began to take off his clothes, wringing the grey water out of them, but soon he stopped that and just sat staring at the ground, as if some important part had been cut out of his brain.

Whatever else you feel about this story, linger over its physical descriptions. The rain, the afternoon, the silent horror of the horse—these to me are almost more real than the room in which I read. Ted Hughes uses the rough, concrete richness of our language—the older English words rather than the smoother Latinate ones—forcefully and exactly. I doubt if you will ever come across a better description of heavy rain in the country.

This said, what are we to make of THE RAIN HORSE? *The rain is real, but what about the horse? In spite of the stone cracking against its flank, and the earth shaking under its charge, you may find evidence for thinking that the horse is an illusion, something created in the man's brain as an image of his special fear and disappointment. (Disappointment at what? Re-read the opening of the story.) It seems, at the end, as if he actually dismisses the horse, with an immense effort—and then, his heart seems "strained", his brain damaged. Is the horse perhaps something to do with the man himself, with his youth in this area!'*

I don't know the answers; yet I like the story. You may find it hard to accept the idea, but a story like this does not have clear answers; the mystery, the fear of the unknown which is rather rare today, is its point. It is no less serious for being shadowy; and if it fascinates you enough to make you want to read it again slowly, if it disturbs and quickens your perceptions in any way, if it stays to advantage in your memory, it has succeeded.

FOR FURTHER READING: The poems of Ted Hughes are exciting and not forbiddingly difficult. You will find them, published by Faber and Faber, in *The Hawk in the Rain, Lupercal, The Earth-Owl and Other Moon People,* and an inexpensive paperback—*Selected Poems of Thom Gunn and Ted Hughes.*

JAMES THURBER

James Thurber, who was born in 1894 and died in 1962, was probably the most popular humorous writer in history, except perhaps for Mark Twain, who was a novelist as well. Both these, and Scott Fitzgerald (see *The Ice Palace*) were Middle-Western Americans. Thurber's humour often has its serious implications, but is always amiable and sympathetic. *The Secret Life of Walter Mitty* is one of the most famous stories of this century, and has often been poorly imitated, but never equalled.

The Secret Life of Walter Mitty

"We're going through!" The Commander's voice was like thin ice breaking. He wore his full-dress uniform, with the heavily braided white cap pulled down rakishly over one cold grey eye. "We can't make it, sir. It's spoiling for a hurricane, if you ask me." "I'm not asking you, Lieutenant Berg," said the Commander. "Throw on the power lights! Rev her up to 8,500! We're going through!" The pounding of the cylinders increased: ta-pocketa-pocketa-pocketa-*pocketa-pocketa*. The Commander stared at the ice forming on the pilot window. He walked over and twisted a row of complicated dials. "Switch on No. 8 auxiliary!" he shouted. "Switch on No. 8 auxiliary!" repeated Lieutenant Berg. "Full strength in No. 3 turret!"

shouted the Commander. "Full strength in No. 3 turret!" The crew, bending to their various tasks in the huge, hurtling eight-engined Navy hydroplane, looked at each other and grinned. "The Old Man'll get us through," they said to one another. "The Old Man ain't afraid of Hell!" . . .

"Not so fast! You're driving too fast!" said Mrs. Mitty. "What are you driving so fast for?"

"Hmmm?" said Walter Mitty. He looked at his wife, in the seat beside him, with shocked astonishment. She seemed grossly unfamiliar, like a strange woman who had yelled at him in a crowd. "You were up to fifty-five," she said. "You know I don't like to go more than forty. You were up to fifty-five." Walter Mitty drove on through Waterbury in silence, the roaring of the SN202 through the worst storm in twenty years of Navy flying fading in the remote, intimate airways of his mind. "You're tensed up again," said Mrs. Mitty. "It's one of your days. I wish you'd let Dr. Renshaw look you over."

Walter Mitty stopped the car in front of the building where his wife went to have her hair done. "Remember to get those overshoes while I'm having my hair done," she said. "I don't need overshoes," said Mitty. She put her mirror back in her bag. "We've been through all that," she said, getting out of the car. "You're not a young man any longer." He raced the engine a little. "Why don't you wear your gloves? Have you lost your gloves?" Walter Mitty reached in a pocket and brought out the gloves. He put them on, but after she had turned and gone into the building and he had driven on to a red light, he took them off again. "Pick it up, brother!" snapped a cop as the light changed, and Mitty hastily pulled on his gloves and lurched ahead. He drove around the streets aimlessly for a time, and then he drove past the hospital on his way to the parking lot.

. . . "It's the millionaire banker, Wellington McMillan,"

said the pretty nurse. "Yes?" said Walter Mitty, removing his gloves slowly. "Who has the case?" "Dr. Renshaw and Dr. Benbow, but there are two specialists here, Dr. Remington from New York and Mr. Pritchard-Mitford from London. He flew over." A door opened down a long, cool corridor and Dr. Renshaw came out. He looked distraught and haggard. "Hello, Mitty," he said. "We're having the devil's own time with McMillan, the millionaire banker and close personal friend of Roosevelt. Obstreosis of the ductal tract. Tertiary. Wish you'd take a look at him." "Glad to," said Mitty.

In the operating room there were whispered introductions: "Dr. Remington, Dr. Mitty. Mr. Pritchard-Mitford, Dr. Mitty." "I've read your book on streptothricosis," said Pritchard-Mitford, shaking hands. "A brilliant performance, sir." "Thank you," said Walter Mitty. "Didn't know you were in the States, Mitty," grumbled Remington. "Coals to Newcastle, bringing Mitford and me up here for a tertiary." "You are very kind," said Mitty. A huge, complicated machine, connected to the operating table, with many tubes and wires, began at this moment to go pocketa-pocketa-pocketa. "The new anaesthetizer is giving way!" shouted an interne. "There is no one in the East who knows how to fix it!" "Quiet, man!" said Mitty, in a low, cool voice. He sprang to the machine, which was now going pocketa-pocketa-queep-pocketa-queep. He began fingering delicately a row of glistening dials. "Give me a fountain pen!" he snapped. Someone handed him a fountain pen. He pulled a faulty piston out of the machine and inserted the pen in its place. "That will hold for ten minutes," he said. "Get on with the operation." A nurse hurried over and whispered to Renshaw, and Mitty saw the man turn pale. "Coreopsis has set in," said Renshaw nervously. "If you would take over, Mitty?" Mitty looked at him and at the craven figure of Benbow, who drank, and at the grave, uncertain faces of the two great specialists. "If you wish," he said. They slipped a white gown on him; he adjusted a mask and drew on thin gloves; nurses handed him shining . . .

"Back it up, Mac! Look out for that Buick!" Walter Mitty jammed on the brakes. "Wrong lane, Mac," said the parking-lot attendant, looking at Mitty closely. "Gee. Yeh," muttered Mitty. He began cautiously to back out of the lane marked "Exit Only". "Leave her sit there," said the attendant. "I'll put her away." Mitty got out of the car. "Hey, better leave the key." "Oh," said Mitty, handing the man the ignition key. The attendant vaulted into the car, backed it up with insolent skill, and put it where it belonged.

They're so damn cocky, thought Walter Mitty, walking along Main Street; they think they know everything. Once he had tried to take his chains off, outside New Milford, and he had got them wound around the axles. A man had had to come out in a wrecking car and unwind them, a young, grinning garageman. Since then Mrs. Mitty always made him drive to a garage to have the chains taken off. The next time, he thought, I'll wear my right arm in a sling; they won't grin at me then. I'll have my right arm in a sling and they'll see I couldn't possibly take the chains off myself. He kicked at the slush on the sidewalk. "Overshoes," he said to himself, and he began looking for a shoe store.

When he came out into the street again, with the overshoes in a box under his arm, Walter Mitty began to wonder what the other thing was his wife had told him to get. She had told him twice, before they set out from their house in Waterbury. In a way he hated these weekly trips to town—he was always getting something wrong. Kleenex, he thought, Squibb's, razor blades? No. Toothpaste, toothbrush, bicarbonate, carborundum, initiative and referendum? He gave it up. But she would remember it. "Where's the what's-its-name?" she would ask. "Don't tell me you forgot the what's-its-name." A news-

boy went by shouting something about the Waterbury trial.
. . . "Perhaps this will refresh your memory." The District
Attorney suddenly thrust a heavy automatic at the quiet figure
on the witness stand. "Have you ever seen this before?"
Walter Mitty took the gun and examined it expertly. "This is
my Webley-Vickers 50.80," he said calmly. An excited buzz
ran round the courtroom. The judge rapped for order. "You
are a crack shot with any sort of firearms, I believe?" said the
District Attorney, insinuatingly. "Objection!" shouted Mitty's
attorney. "We have shown that the defendant could not have
fired the shot. We have shown that he wore his right arm in a
sling on the night of the fourteenth of July." Walter Mitty
raised his hand briefly and the bickering attorneys were stilled.
"With any known make of gun," he said evenly, "I could have
killed Gregory Fitzhurst at three hundred feet *with my left
hand*." Pandemonium broke loose in the courtroom. A
woman's scream rose above the bedlam and suddenly a lovely,
dark-haired girl was in Walter Mitty's arms. The District
Attorney struck at her savagely. Without rising from his chair,
Mitty let the man have it on the point of the chin, "You
miserable cur!" . . .

"Puppy biscuit," said Walter Mitty. He stopped walking
and the buildings of Waterbury rose up out of the misty
courtroom and surrounded him again. A woman who was
passing laughed. "He said 'Puppy biscuit'," she said to her
companion. "That man said 'Puppy biscuit' to himself."
Walter Mitty hurried on. He went into an A and P., not the
first one he came to but a smaller one farther up the street. "I
want some biscuit for small, young dogs," he said to the clerk.
"Any special brand, sir?" The greatest pistol shot in the world
thought for a moment. "It says 'Puppies bark for It' on the
box," said Walter Mitty.

His wife would be through at the hairdresser's in fifteen

minutes, Mitty saw in looking at his watch, unless they had trouble drying it; sometimes they had trouble drying it. She didn't like to get to the hotel first; she would want him to be there waiting for her as usual. He found a big leather chair in the lobby, facing a window, and he put the overshoes and the puppy biscuit on the floor beside it. He picked up an old copy of *Liberty* and sank down into the chair. "Can Germany Conquer the World Through the Air?" Walter Mitty looked at the pictures of bombing planes and of ruined streets.

. . . "The cannonading has got the wind up in young Raleigh, sir," said the sergeant. Captain Mitty looked up at him through tousled hair. "Get him to bed," he said wearily. "With the others. I'll fly alone." "But you can't, sir," said the sergeant anxiously. "It takes two men to handle that bomber and the Archies are pounding hell out of the air. Von Richtman's circus is between here and Saulier." "Somebody's got to get that ammunition dump," said Mitty. "I'm going over. Spot of brandy?" He poured a drink for the sergeant and one for himself. War thundered and whined around the dugout and battered at the door. There was a rending of wood and splinters flew through the room. "A bit of a near thing," said Captain Mitty carelessly. "The box barrage is closing in," said the sergeant. "We only live once, Sergeant," said Mitty, with his faint, fleeting smile. "Or do we?" He poured another brandy and tossed it off. "I never see a man could hold his brandy like you, sir," said the sergeant. "Begging your pardon, sir." Captain Mitty stood up and strapped on his huge Webley-Vickers automatic. "It's forty kilometres through hell, sir," said the sergeant. Mitty finished one last brandy. "After all," he said softly, "what isn't?" The pounding of the cannon increased; there was the rat-tat-tatting of machine-guns, and from somewhere came the menacing pocketa-pocketa-pocketa of the new flame-throwers. Walter Mitty walked to the door

of the dugout humming "Aupres de ma Blonde". He turned
and waved to the sergeant. "Cheerio!" he said. . . .

Something struck his shoulder. "I've been looking all over
this hotel for you," said Mrs. Mitty. "Why do you have to
hide in this old chair? How did you expect me to find you?"
"Things close in," said Walter Mitty vaguely. "What?" Mrs.
Mitty said. "Did you get the what's-its-name? The puppy
biscuit? What's in that box?" "Overshoes," said Mitty.
"Couldn't you have put them on in the store?" "I was thinking," said Walter Mitty. "Does it ever occur to you that
sometimes I am thinking?" She looked at him. "I'm going to
take your temperature when I get you home," she said.

They went out through the revolving doors that made a
faintly derisive whistling sound when you pushed them. It was
two blocks to the parking lot. At the drugstore on the corner
she said, "Wait here for me. I forgot something. I won't be a
minute." She was more than a minute. Walter Mitty lighted a
cigarette. It began to rain, rain with sleet in it. He stood up
against the wall of the drugstore, smoking. . . . He put his
shoulders back and his heels together. "To hell with the handkerchief," said Walter Mitty scornfully. He took one last drag
on his cigarette and snapped it away. Then with that faint,
fleeting smile playing about his lips, he faced the firing squad;
erect and motionless, proud and disdainful, Walter Mitty the
Undefeated, inscrutable to the last.

*This is a story that can be quickly enjoyed at one reading;
but you may now like to return and notice the skill with which
James Thurber imitates the style of popular fiction of various
sorts, right down to the hackneyed and often stupid phrases of
supposed "glory" or "romance". Some readers may like to
add episodes to this story, or to write their own versions, about
a modern boy or girl Mitty.*

The Secret Life of Walter Mitty

Walter Mitty might be called an "escapist". Escaping from what? How far would you defend his right to do so?

FOR FURTHER READING: Almost anything by James Thurber (who draws his own pictures as well), but particularly *The Thurber Carnival*, Hamish Hamilton and Penguin.

JAMES HANLEY

Though he has never achieved wide popularity, Hanley has for years been recognized as a writer of distinction and integrity. His novels and stories vary considerably in their subject-matter, but several, like *The Road*, are concerned with men returned from the sea, and with the lives and feelings of ordinary people, of whom he writes with deep sympathy.

The Road

When the pilot said "steady", Elsen said quietly, "steady she goes, sir", keeping his eye fast on the point, then he lost it, the whole world was rocking in the binnacle. And he could not hold it. It had been like this since he heard the first ring of the bell, and knew that the land lay to port. For a moment he could not believe it but the bell struck again, and suddenly he had it, the shape and feel and smell of the land.

"Where I was born," he said, "where I was born."

"Starboard a point," the pilot said, against wind, out of a muffled mouth.

"Starboard a point it is, sir," Elsen said, whilst the world rocked in the binnacle, and memories rose like waves, came to him like gusts of wind and streaks of lightning, the last notes of songs. The ship rode steady under his hand, nearer to the land.

"Port a point."

"Port a point, sir," Elsen said, he never looked up.

The bridge dodger came up suddenly with the crack of whips, but he did not hear it. He watched the compass point and he tried to remember. Ten years. A long time. Six years of war, in all oceans, in every sea. A long time.

"Steady."

"Steady she goes, sir."

"There's dad."

"Mum."

"Phyllis. I wonder what she's like," and the name came warm and soft to his tongue.

His brothers.

His sisters.

"I wrote them. I always did."

"They wrote back, too. Never failed."

"Phyllis'll be just thirty. Makes you feel old. Funny they stopped writing."

His heart gave a sudden leap. "What matter. I'm home."

Feeling the land, smelling it, seeing it out of all-devouring eyes.

"Port a bit," the pilot said.

"Port a bit it is, sir," Elsen said, watching Phyllis dancing in the binnacle, heard Dad's farewell, Mum's call.

"I'm old, too. Thirty. Seems strange. Everything does. Not quite real, not quite normal."

"Had a rough passage they say," remarked the pilot.

"Yes, sir. A bit rough these last days."

O'Rourke came behind him, saying: "O.K., John. Clear out."

"Right," Elsen said, watched O'Rourke take over, then went away, his gait aimless, indeterminate, moving clumsily down the companion ladder, glaring out at the sea, the un-believable land, hurrying up the well deck, vanishing up the fo'c'sle alleyway. Noise in the fo'c'sle, a cloud of smoke, raised voices, the periodic roar of wind in the chain-locker, the thud of the sea. He climbed into his bunk, he dragged open the port, put his head through and looked. And saw nothing and heard nothing and felt nothing. He knelt there, very quiet, very still, his body moving gently to the ship's rhythm. Tins rolled across the fo'c'sle floor, white canvas bags were filling, a sailor was singing.

"After two years things'll be a bit different," a voice said.

A boy laughed, wrapped up his present for his girl, went on laughing.

Outside a thousand white horses were racing towards the land, Elsen watched them fly by, watched grey cloud scud across his horizon line. The sea was bright green.

"Dad, and Mum, and Phyllis and Frank and Jill, Tom and Bill."

Elsen turned away from the port-hole, climbed down to the deck, pulled his empty bag after him and started to pack it.

"They say she'll be tied up before noon," the boy said.

And Elsen said, "So they say," and the words seemed to fall as heavy as lead into the empty bag.

"There'll be a whole fortnight ashore at least, so I've heard," a man said.

"So I hear," Elsen said, stuffing clothes into the bag.

He pushed in a heavy pair of leather sea-boots. "Am I dreaming?"

"All hands out there," the bosun cried down the alleyway, "all hands out."

There was the land, the familiar building looming up. Elsen went to the rail and looked. "Yes, this is it, this is where I was born. Ten years, it does seem a long time, and then it doesn't, somehow——" turning away, following the rest of the watch up to the fo'c'sle head.

Somewhere in the distance, through the mist, a tug blew, two tugs were moving down on her.

"Bound to know, they're bound to know," Elsen kept repeating to himself, "always remembered, always followed the move of my ships, every day in the shipping paper. They'll be there, someone will be there."

Guessing who, wondering if it might be *her*, Phyllis on his tongue again, whilst he stood by with the others, a heaving-line coiled and ready in his hand. "Might even be all of them. Good Lord! Never thought of that. Like that time I made my first trip. They all came. They were standing on the quay, watching for me. I was on the poop."

High right hand came up, swung, and the line flew outwards. A burst of steam from the windlass, the great rópe began to pay out to the tug. He watched the fast approaching waterfront, the docks, he heard voices behind him.

"Fortnight at the least, I should say, after a long trip like we've done."

"On the other hand she might turn round right away. Never can tell these times."

Quietly, casually, the bosun said, "You can go below, you and you and *you*, I'll call you later."

Elsen followed the two men down the ladder.

"He's trying his damnedest to be decent on this last day of the trip," O'Rourke said.

"It must be a hard fight for him, I'm sure," Grey said.

Elsen had nothing to say. In the fo'c'sle he went on with his packing, whistling a tune through his teeth, wondering who would be there.

"There's the gangway gone up," O'Rourke said. "This man's ship is in."

Elsen made a knot in his bag, then went out on deck. He stood leaning on the rail: people were coming down the quay, men and women, children, babies in arms. Through the dock shed came officials, customs, Dock board, dockers. Elsen scanned every new face. Men were already passing down the gangway, their bags and suitcases high on their shoulders. He heard shouts, laughter. "I'll wait a bit," Elsen thought, "a bit longer."

Then he watched them go, after the shouts, the laughter, the kisses, one group after another.

"Well! They haven't come. It is strange. Expected somebody. *One* of them, anyhow. Ah well," moving away, dragging his feet up the fo'c'sle alleyway.

"Perhaps I'm dreaming after all, in a minute I'll wake up."

He picked up his bag, and went out on deck, hoping and not hoping. The quay was bare, silent.

"Ah well."

He went off up to the shed.

And on the dock road he stopped suddenly, dropped his bag to his feet. It was hard to believe. But this was no dream. This was true. This was home. He was bewildered, sad, uncertain, he watched the heavy traffic stream by. He saw a pub called "The Rose and Crown". He remembered this. He picked up his bag and went inside. The faces were new, he didn't know them. Sitting down, he called for a drink.

"Just docked?"

The barman was short, stout, cheery. "Nice drop of rain."

"Just docked," Elsen said, "bring me a small whisky."

"Been away long?"

"Ten years," he said. "Thanks."

"Phew!" the barman exclaimed, "that's a hell of a trip."

"This ship was away two years," Elsen said.

He glanced around the bar. It was dark. The dull morning put a blur on brass, on the rows of brightly labelled bottles.

"A 15A tram takes you to Saunders Road from here?" Elsen said.

"I should think it does," the barman replied, not knowing.

Elsen picked up his bag, "morning," he struggled through the door.

He dropped the bag to his feet, he looked up the road for a tram. There was none in sight. But the road was choked with heavy lorries, loaded and unloaded, horse-drawn vehicles, cars, bicycles. The noise deafened him. "It is curious," he thought, "and then the letters stopping. Maybe they've moved, maybe they did write and the ship left port before they arrived, maybe——" and then he saw the tram, its garish colours of red and green, saw the top-heavy vehicle lurching towards him.

"They've not changed anyhow, good old warhorses those trams."

He hailed the driver and the tram stopped. He climbed aboard, saying quietly to the conductor, "Not in your way, I hope," jamming his bag in behind the stairs. "You can give me my ticket now. Saunders Road."

"Saunders Road?" said the conductor.

"That's it. Fourpence, isn't it?"

"Never heard of Saunders Road," the conductor said.

"Then god damn," Elsen said angrily, "what country am I in? How long you been on this job?"

"Eighteen months, but I never heard of that road. Tell you what. Take a tuppenny to the centre of the city, anybody'll know after that." He pushed the ticket in the sailor's hand, and Elsen went upstairs. But he did not sit down. He glared wildly through the window, crossing the deck, glaring out on the other side, he was suddenly afraid to sit down.

He laughed. "Born here, and yet I don't know where I am."

Then he sat down and waited. Phyllis came in his mind again, Mum, Dad, the others. It was strange nobody had come to meet him. Now, on this tram, tearing its way towards the city, its bells clanging continuously to clear traffic from the line, he felt lost, sad, angry, he longed for a face he knew. The

81

tram stopped, more passengers came up. A woman and three children passed down in front of him. The children were noisy, their laughter hard, it irritated the sailor sitting behind them.

"Excuse me, lady," he said, "does this tram go to Saunders Road?"

"Saunders Road. I don't think so, that is, no I'm sure it doesn't. Have you asked the conductor?" She turned round, beamed on him.

He liked her fat red face, her jolly laughing eyes.

"I've already asked him."

"Oh dear," she said.

Elsen sat back in his seat. "Guess it'll turn up," forcing a laugh, "guess it'll turn up."

"Do you live there?"

"Yes. That's why I'm going there of course. Just come home off a trip."

"Oh, I see. Wish I could help, but I'm afraid I've never heard of the road."

The conductor bawled up to him. "You get off here."

Elsen hurried down the iron stairs. He picked up his bag, the conductor caught his arm, "Steady chum, this isn't the Atlantic Ocean," he said, watched the lorry rush forward, then helped the sailor down with the bag.

Elsen stepped into the street, it was like stepping into the maelstrom.

He stood there staring round him. He tried to move, but his feet seemed weighted with lead, he pressed his two hands on the neck of the bag. People streamed past, they barely noticed him. In a seaport a sailor is not noticed.

"Can I help you?"

Elsen looked up, startled. A policeman was standing in front of him.

"Thanks. Could you tell me the right numbered tram to take me to Saunders Road?"

"Saunders Road?"

Elsen felt he wanted to screech. Was everybody deaf?

"That's it," he shouted, "SAUNDERS ROAD."

"Just a minute," the policeman said, pulling a small directory from his pocket. "I believe I can help you. Been away
long?"

"Ten years," the sailor said.

"Ah! I thought you looked a bit lost," the policeman said,
muttered under his breath, "Saunders Road, Saunders Road,
Sau-unders—. That's odd. I can't see it in this directory. Yet
this is the latest one. Half a minute. Give me the name of any
other road near it, that'll help."

"Hornby Road."

"Hornby Road," muttered the policeman.

Saunders Road, the sailor was saying, was a very long,
narrow road, a steep road all the way.

"Hornby Road. Here we are," the policeman said, his smile
was triumphant. "Now we're moving. Take a 12B tram to
Sisters Road, get off there, cut down Sisters Road, take a
sharp turn left and there you are."

He pushed the book back in his pocket. "Look, there's a
12B now. Just pulled up."

He took the sailor's arm, piloted him across the road.

"Thanks," Elsen said, "thanks very much, officer."

He climbed aboard, and again he jammed the bag in behind
the stairs, "Won't be in your way?" he asked the conductor.

"Nothing ever gets in my way," the conductor said, "where
to?"

"Sisters Road."

"Threepence."

"Thank you," Elsen said, this time he went and sat on the
lower deck.

"I'm disappointed, I know I am, I did expect one of them to
meet me. Hell, I could walk all the way to Saunders Road, and

83

know every street, every turning, walk to it with my eyes shut. They must have altered the tram routes. Curious the way nobody seemed to know. Good job that policeman turned up. Decent." He sat quietly in his seat, fiddled with a heavy gold signet ring on the little finger of his left hand. "I wonder what Phyllis is like?

"Mum's fat, but she always was. Dad long and stringy. Always looked odd together. Tom'll be twenty-two now. Sometimes it seems like a hundred years, sometimes it's just minutes. *God*, it'll be good to see them." He felt less lost, less sad, he began to understand, there were reasons why they could not come down to meet him. The whole thing was clarified.

"Shipping paper's got it all wrong. Besides we're in two days earlier than we hoped to be."

Hope rose, he smiled to himself.

"Sisters Road."

"At last," he thought. "At last. Now I can say I'm home."

He waited till an old man got off, then picked up the bag. He stepped down from the tram. He waited to see it move off, then crossed the street. "Here we are," he said, "down here. Now I know. What a fool I am. Fancy me not remembering the road I was born in."

He whistled his way down Sisters Road, his bag as light as air, his pace brisk, he thought of the surprise for them, he thought of one hundred and one Saunders Road, he thought of home. At the bottom he stopped.

"Turn left."

He turned and walked on. He saw a street of eight houses, and then the wilderness.

"Hornby Road," he said, "where the hell's Hornby Road?"

A woman was cleaning her step. He went up to her.

"Excuse me, lady, am I right for Saunders Road?"

She looked at him for a while without speaking. She realized at once that he had just come off a ship.

"I must be crazy today, don't know my way about. Not even where I belong."

"Belong?"

He stared at her.

"Where do you belong?" she asked him.

The bag fell at his feet, he could not speak, he could not understand.

"This is a bit of Hornby Road," the woman said, "and that was Saunders Road."

Elsen did not move. He felt something swimming inside him, he said, "I——"

"You had better come in," the woman said, she put a hand on the sailor's arm. She called into the house, "Fred, come quick, will you."

And when Fred came, "He was looking for Saunders Road and he was standing on it all the while," she said.

"Oh!" Fred said, "Oh!"

Elsen had fallen across his canvas bag. They took him into the house.

"It's quite upset me so it has," Mrs. Gurney said, "I peeped round the door to see how he was, but he wasn't asleep. He was lying flat on his back, his eyes wide open, staring up at the ceiling. He's such a fine big man, it did upset me."

"What's he going to do?" asked Fred.

"I don't know."

"Have to do something, I suppose."

"Who is he, has he said anything yet?"

"A bit," the woman said, "not much. His name's Elsen. John Elsen. He's just come back off a two years' trip. Altogether he's been away from here ten years. He lived in Saunders Road. He was born there. His girl lived in one hundred and thirty-three. His father and mother, two brothers and a sister, they all lived in one hundred and one. But I said I didn't know anybody of that name."

"Couldn't very well," Fred said, "since we've only been living here a year ourselves. But I expect they'll turn up somehow or other, some of them anyhow, people have a remarkable way of turning up."

"They do—sometimes, don't they," she replied.

"What a lousy homecoming," Fred said.

"I'll slip up and see if he's asleep."

She found Elsen sitting on the bed, leaning forward, his hands clasped, staring out through the window. She quietly closed the door and crept downstairs again.

What Elsen was staring at was a bare hill that ran down sheer to the river, to the very frontiers of the sea. The long narrow road, with its two lines of squat houses huddled together, as though out of some desperate loyalty to each other to keep the light shut out. The six shops and the church. He stared at this long bare hill, at the forest of masts in the distance, he remembered how as a child he had so often stared from a bedroom window, especially in the evening when the buzzers sounded, and the long road was suddenly full of men making their way up from the docks, a dense mass of men climbing the hill; it was as though some large black cloud had fallen earthwards. Watching the cloud move, explode and split up, watching for his father.

"Are you asleep, Mr. Elsen?"

Fred was standing inside the door.

Elsen turned and looked at the man.

"Better come on down, chum," Fred said, "we've a meal ready. Come along now."

He waited till the sailor got up, he put his arm through his, he led him from the room like a child, he whispered encouraging things as they went downstairs.

"You never slept," the woman said, as soon as he put his head inside the door, a direct accusation.

They sat down, Elsen at the far end of the table by the door.

But he did not eat, and he did not speak. Suddenly he was crying and they stopped eating.

"I can't believe it," he blurted out, "I can't believe it." Fred looked down at his boots, his wife stared over the sailor's head, the clock's tick was suddenly louder.

"I know," the woman said, "I know."

Speaking under his breath, his eye still fixed on the carpet, Fred said, "Know what?"

"I know," she said, got up from the table and went upstairs. When she came down again she was dressed to go out.

"I won't be long."

Nobody spoke, nobody looked at her, she went out and the door banged behind her.

"Chum!" said Fred.

"You must eat something," Fred said, "you must."

"Always they used to come down and meet me," Elsen said, "always."

"Yes, I understand, chum, I understand. Don't think I don't."

He looked at the tall, broad-shouldered man with the thick brown hair, the weather-beaten face with a scar running down from the right ear to the base of the neck, the grey eyes under the bushy brows, one big hand resting on the table, a small tattooed star lying at the base of the thumb.

"I don't know what to say to him," thought Fred, "I really don't. It's plain awful."

"Cheer up, chum," he blurted out, "something'll happen." He felt relieved when he heard the front door opening and his wife came in. Fred looked at her, she did not speak, she took her hat and coat off, handed them to her husband, "Take them upstairs, Fred," she said, "then go to 'The Mermaid' and bring me back a little whisky. You'll find the little bottle in the back kitchen cupboard."

She waited for him to go. She stood motionless, Fred came down again, went into the back kitchen. The woman sat down the moment he went out.

"Mr. Elsen," she said.

He found her sitting beside him.

"I've found a gentleman who will be able to help you. Nobody round here can. Nobody who ever lived here two years ago lives here now. But this gentleman can help. He's a priest. His name is Father Tumilty. He used to be at St. Sebastian's church here. Go to him. He may be able to tell you something," she paused, suddenly put her hand on his hand, "I'm sorry," she said.

"Have you any relations at all, Mr. Elsen?" asked Mrs. Gurney.

"Only an aunt," he said.

"Oh! That helps a bit, doesn't it?"

"She had the end house in Hornby Road," Elsen said.

"Oh!——" Mrs. Gurney exclaimed, "oh!——"

Fred came back. She was glad. He poured out some whisky and gave it to the sailor.

"Have a drop yourself, Fred, just for company's sake."

"Righto."

"Your very good health, chum," Fred said, he glanced across at his wife. "What was it you knew?"

"It just came into my head a minute ago. Remember Father Tumilty, that priest, lives at the end of Sisters Road now, since St. Sebastian's went. Well, he was in Saunders Road that night, he'd know something. It's not far from here, Mr. Elsen, I feel sure he could help you. Knew everybody in this neighbourhood. I'll show you the way," she said, "I'll take you up there. Try not to be too downhearted, Mr. Elsen, you never know——"

"It's hard to find the right thing to say," she thought, "hard to find, but easy to say. I wish I could help. Never saw anybody so lost-looking, never."

"We only just come to live here twelve months ago," Fred said, "had our place down on top of us. They got everything 'cept the bloody mice."

"Fred!"

"When you're ready," she said quietly, and immediately Fred got up.

"I'll take him," he said.

"You stay here," she said. "I can see to this."

Fred patted the sailor on the back as he got up.

"Wouldn't give up hope chum, try not to. Nothing after that's gone," following Elsen into the lobby, standing awkwardly behind the front door, waiting for his wife to come out, wondering what he could say, feeling tongue-tied, thinking, "Lousy, coming home like that," suddenly blurted out, "Best of luck."

Mrs. Gurney came to the door. She opened it and Elsen stepped into the street.

"Hope something happens," Fred said.

He shut the door, went into the parlour, watched them through the window.

"Lived in Saunders Road, eh, fine bloody road it is now," thought Fred, went back to the kitchen, he thought there was a drop of whisky left in the bottle.

"All the way down here they had it," Mrs. Gurney said, "church used to be *there*. That was a grocer's once," pointing, "all the way down they had it. Two land mines together. Awful everywhere then, ten days and nights of it. I thought the world was really coming to an end. But oh, the relief when it was over," and suddenly warming to the thought, "it's wonderful."

Elsen walked by her side, over the rubble, across the desert. He listened, she talked on and on, growing more voluble, he remained silent. They went slowly on, down the long hill, towards the river, towards the very frontiers of the sea. Once she stopped and looked at him.

"Are you all right?"

"I'm all right."

"It used to look just like a long tunnel down to the sea," he said to himself, and in a moment the houses were back, clutched and clutching, shutting out sky, the church, the shops, the bell ringing, the sound of sirens from the ships lying in the docks, he saw them clearly now, lying under mist in the winter evenings, holding the walled-in torpor of high summer nights.

"This way."

He turned as she turned, moved along, the road seemed to have no end.

"See that house over there," Mrs. Gurney said. "There, with the green door."

"I see."

"That's it. Can't come no farther, sorry, got to get my husband ready for the night shift. Come back and tell us how you get on. I do hope something will turn up for you. Anything we can do to help," she said.

"Thanks very much," the sailor said, "you're very good."

She watched him walk away, across the road, saw him ring the bell.

The door opened, he went inside. Mrs. Gurney retraced her steps homeward.

"Well?" Fred said, as soon as she got in the door.

"Oh, it's hopeless really, I knew it the moment he said the name of the road. . . ."

"It made me feel quite sick," she said suddenly, and Fred

said, "Here, have this little drop that's left. What a shock for him."

"Did you really think you were being funny, talking about mice?"

"I don't know."

"Well you weren't."

When the green door opened, the sailor saw a woman looking out at him. She was dressed entirely in black.

"Yes?"

"Could I see the priest, please, a Father Tumilty, that's the name, I think."

"That's right. Is it urgent?"

She watched him carefully, as he put one foot on the top step, cautiously she kept the door only half open.

"It is urgent," the sailor said.

She threw back the door. "Please come inside. I'll find him. He's somewhere about the house. Wait in there."

She showed him into a small study, then went away.

Elsen looked at rows and rows of books, at a blue marble clock on the table in the window.

"Good evening."

He looked up, and as the priest came in he stood to his feet.

"Good evening, sir—I mean Father."

Father Tumilty was eighty-four, very frail, a tiny man, the sailor helped him to a chair. He had not expected to see one so old as this.

"Thank you. What is it you want?"

"I was sent here to see if you could help me," Elsen said.

"Speak up."

"I was sent here to see if you could HELP ME."

"Who are you?"

"My name's Elsen," the sailor said.

"What's that?"

"Elsen, my name's Elsen. ELSEN."

"Oh!—I see," a long pause, "please speak up, sir."

The sailor raised his voice again, "Looking for my family, can't find them," shouting louder without realizing it, "used to live in Saunders Road. SAUNDERS ROAD."

"Oh!—I see," Father Tumilty said.

The sailor on the opposite chair still remained a dark blur.

"Trying to find them," Elsen stammered out, "name's ELSEN."

The door opened and the housekeeper came in. She went straight up to the sailor, motioned to him to follow her out.

Standing in the hall outside, she spoke quietly to him.

"Father Tumilty is old, very very old, very tired. Can I help you?"

Elsen began again, the same words, the same gestures, the technique of despair.

"Oh! I *am* sorry. I wish I could help you, Mr. Elsen. It is true that Father Tumilty was in Saunders Road that night, he was in a shelter administering to the dying. But he remembers nothing, nothing at all, he's so old, it was just noise to him."

She paused for a moment, then her practical mind came to the rescue. "There's always the police."

"No, no, not yet." the sailor said, "not yet."

"Do you know where Sisters Road is?" she asked Elsen.

"I know Sisters Road," he said.

"Well then——" she paused again, looked curiously at Elsen's face, "well, then, at the very bottom there is a small general shop kept by a Mr. Herron. *He* may be able to help you. He was a Warden in the Road and was on duty that particular night. I remember it. He is an old man, but not so old as Father Tumilty, he has a good memory, especially for names. He'll remember *that*."

"I'm very grateful to you," Elsen said, "thank you very much," and very awkwardly he put out his hand, which she took and shook. "I do hope everything will be all right for you," she said, and led him out.

She stood watching him cross the street, "the poor creature". She closed the door.

Elsen turned into Sisters Road and walked quickly down. He found the shop and stopped, staring up at the window. It was a parlour shop, there were muslin curtains on the windows. He saw brightly coloured dummy boxes of a famous soap, piled high. He hesitated on the step, and when finally he opened the door and the bell clanged loudly he did not hear it. He stood in the middle of the shop, waiting. It was very quiet. When Mr. Herron came out he did not notice him. He stood motionless, staring at a shelf packed with patent medicines.

"Well?" Mr. Herron said.

He was seventy, short, and on the stout side. His shaggy hair was uncombed, he had a white muffler round his throat, and was in his shirt sleeves. The bottom buttons of the waistcoat were open, revealing the large shining buckle of a belt. It was this buckle that caught Elsen's eye. He realized in a moment that the owner of the shop was there, staring at him.

"Good evening," the sailor said.

"Evenin'," Mr. Herron replied, and somewhat abruptly, "what do you want?"

"Are you Mr. Herron?"

"That's me all right."

"I wonder if you could help me," Elsen said.

"Help you? Are you begging?"

He came right up to the counter and stared at the sailor.

"A Father Tumilty sent me down here, I'm——"

"Oh him!" and for some reason known only to himself Mr. Herron burst out laughing. "Well, and what can I do for you?"

He looked suspiciously at Elsen, and quite unconsciously pushed in the cash drawer and turned the key in the lock.

"My name's Elsen. I've just come home from sea today. I've——"

"Yes," Mr. Herron interrupted, "go on."

"I'm looking for my people."

"Who's your people?"

"The Elsens. They used to live in Saunders Road. I made sure somebody'd be down to meet me when I docked this morning. Always came down to meet me. Then I took a tram and went up to Saunders Road and it wasn't there."

"Saunders Road. I should think it blinkinwell wasn't there. What then?"

Elsen looked blankly at Mr. Herron, he seemed to be struggling to say something, and at last he blurted out, "I don't know."

"You don't know, don't know what?"

"I don't know where my family is, I can't find them. Course I know about what happened, heard it when I was at sea, and when I got in this morning—crooked streets, spaces and that."

"Well then?"

"The housekeeper at Father Tumilty's said you were a warden in Saunders Road that night. Said you might be able to help me."

Mr. Herron watched the sailor put both hands on his counter, he saw the fingers stretch and press upon the wood, he saw a fist clench suddenly, begin a slow drumming, he heard the sailor say: "Can you help me?"

"Ah!" Mr. Herron said, "what you really want is information on what happened that night. I see now. Will you come this way," he came round from the counter, "just follow me," he said.

The sailor followed Mr. Herron into a kitchen. He found Mr. Herron a very active man, with a bright, alert mind, even at seventy.

"Just sit there," Mr. Herron said, offering him a well-scrubbed chair, whilst he himself sat at the end of the table. It was covered with a green tablecloth, a plant pot stood in the centre on a large blue saucer, its leaves faded brown at the tops. The kitchen, like the shop, smelt strongly of soap, paraffin, candles, cheap boiled sweets.

Mr. Herron began nipping off the faded ends of the plant, he had a good look at Elsen, he leaned forward, spread his bare arms on the table. His manner changed.

"Yes, sir. I was a warden that night, every night. Remember Saunders Road, remember it well. I'm one of the few wardens that kept records," there was a note of triumph in his voice, "I may be able to give you the information you're looking for."

He got up and crossed over to a cupboard set in the wall, he pulled out one drawer after another, he kept up a flow of conversation.

Elsen stared at his broad back.

"Yes, that's one thing I did do. I kept records. There were wardens and wardens. If I hadn't kept them records I mightn't have been able to help at all. Every night, soon's the All Clear went, I got out me book, recorded everything. The authorities were very obliged to me, very obliged. Ah! Here we are now," he exclaimed, and returned to the table and sat down. He opened the book in the middle and laid it flat.

"See," he said, "every street, every road, every alley, every house, every shelter, *all* cellars. Everything down. Now I might be able to help. Saunders Road. Name Elsen."

The sailor sat very still, he was unable to speak.

"Here we are, sir. Saunders Road. Got it. October 18th, 1941. Give it you word for word, here it is. 'Heard the horns go off and looked at my watch. Half past five. Punctual to the minute. Dead on time. Like they always are. Arrived Post A five thirty-two. Sent out Jones and Hughes check up on inventories. All occupants checked, found correct. Heavy stuff at seven thirty-eight. 'Phone rang and I got orders to rush to

Post B, bad incident. In the fifteen minutes I was at Post B two land mines came down on Saunders Road. Ordered there. Went back at once. Very bad incident. Not even a cat left. Checked inventories. Four-ten. Finished counting. Two hundred and seventy-three bodies. Time four-twelve. Signed. George Herron.' "

Suddenly he looked at Elsen.

"What's the name again, slipped my mind."

"El-el-el-el——"

"Ah!" Mr. Herron said, "I see. H'm! Look up the E's."

He skipped through the pages. "Elsen."

Elsen lowered his eyes.

"Mrs. Mary Elsen.

"Mr. Tom Elsen.

"Miss May Elsen.

"Miss Jill Elsen.

"Joseph Elsen.

"William Elsen.

"Miss Phyllis Wright.

"Mrs. Ann Shore.

"Eight."

He shut the book.

"Never did no harm to anybody," Elsen burst out, "never——"

Mr. Herron got up. He crossed over to the sailor.

"I'm very sorry, Mr. Elsen, very sorry, world we live in, innocence doesn't mean nothing at all. Anything I can do——"

Elsen sat up, looked at Mr. Herron.

"No thanks—very—good—you——"

He went clumsily into the shop, banged his knee against the counter. "——'night."

"Good night, Mr. Elsen."

The door closed, the bell tinkled on.

"If I hadn't kept them records like I did, he'd never have

96

found out what happened. Bad case, very bad case."
Elsen picked up his bag and went back to the ship.

This is a carefully written story and we should not let its simplicity deceive us. The shuffling, broken way in which Elsen, and the people he meets, think and speak and move, is captured very closely, and it becomes the way in which the whole story is expressed. I find that any impatience or bewilderment I feel at moments when things seem long-drawn-out or confused, are more than made up for by the feeling of reality which the story creates. James Hanley never exaggerates, but he is not afraid to say, where it is true, that the sailor "was crying"; his people are not in any way artificial, "fictional" people, but like ourselves and those whom we meet every day; neither better nor worse. The length, and the baldness, of the story are necessary to make us feel, as if we were Elsen ourselves, how total is his loss.

Why does the author spend time showing us Elsen on board ship, with his fellow sailors?

When Elsen gets ashore and begins his muddle with the trams, what details show that he has been a long time at sea? Why does the conductor of the first tram catch his arm as he is getting off?

The maelstrom was a mythical ocean whirlpool of which sailors were once terrified. Why does it appear in this story?

Why doesn't Mrs. Gurney go all the way to Father Tumilty's (what is her real *reason)?*

What feelings does Mr. Herron really have, as he sees Elsen out at the end? Is the writer being unfair here, or just honest?

Notice the behaviour of the people Elsen meets: the barman, the two tram conductors, the lady on the tram, the policeman, Mrs. Gurney and her husband, Father Tumilty's housekeeper,

Mr. Herron. Some are more sympathetic than others, but all are willing to help up to a point—and no further. It is doubtful whether this is meanness, or a sort of fear (not wanting to poke one's nose in too far); whatever it is, it's something the British are particularly accused of. What do you feel?

JOYCE CARY

Joyce Cary was a man, and this was his real name. When he died in 1957, he had become accepted widely as one of our best modern novelists. He wrote about many different things —Africa, children, painters and their lives—but always with generosity and a sharp intelligence. In this story, which is told without tricks of style or fireworks of any kind, many readers will be amused to recognize themselves; but Cary shows us that "growing up", whether at thirteen or at fifty-two, can be a disconcerting challenge.

Growing Up

Robert Quick, coming home after a business trip, found a note from his wife. She would be back at four, but the children were in the garden. He tossed down his hat, and still in his dark business suit, which he disliked very much, made at once for the garden.

He had missed his two small girls and looked forward eagerly to their greeting. He had hoped indeed that they might, as often before, have been waiting at the corner of the road, to flag the car, and drive home with him.

The Quicks' garden was a wilderness. Except for a small vegetable patch near the pond, and one bed where Mrs. Quick

99

grew flowers for the house, it had not been touched for years. Old apple trees tottered over seedy laurels, unpruned roses. Tall ruins of dahlias and delphiniums hung from broken sticks.

The original excuse for this neglect was that the garden was for the children. They should do what they liked there. The original truth was that neither of the Quicks cared for gardening. Besides, Mrs. Quick was too busy with family, council, and parish affairs, Quick with his office, to give time to a hobby that bored them both.

But the excuse had become true. The garden belonged to the children, and Quick was even proud of it. He would boast of his wild garden, so different from any neighbour's shaved grass and combed beds. It had come to seem, for him, a triumph of imagination; and this afternoon, once more, he found it charming in its wildness, an original masterpiece among gardens.

And, in fact, with the sun just warming up in mid-May, slanting steeply past the trees, and making even old weeds shine red and gold, it had the special beauty of untouched woods, where there is still, even among closely farmed lands, a little piece of free nature left, a suggestion of the frontier, primeval forests.

"A bit of real wild country," thought Quick, a townsman for whom the country was a place for picnics. And he felt at once released, escaped. He shouted, "Hullo, hullo, children."

There was no answer. And he stopped, in surprise. Then he thought, "They've gone to meet me—I've missed them." And this gave him both pleasure and dismay. The last time the children had missed him, two years before, having gone a mile down the road and lain in ambush behind a hedge, there had been tears. They had resented being searched for, and brought home; they had hated the humiliating failure of their surprise.

But even as he turned back towards the house, and dodged

a tree, he caught sight of Jenny, lying on her stomach by the pond, with a book under her nose. Jenny was twelve and had lately taken furiously to reading.

Quick made for the pond with long steps, calling, "Hullo, hullo, Jenny, hullo," waving. But Jenny merely turned her head slightly and peered at him through her hair. Then she dropped her cheek on the book as if to say, "Excuse me, it's really too hot."

And now he saw Kate, a year older. She was sitting on the swing, leaning sideways against a rope, with her head down, apparently in deep thought. Her bare legs, blotched with mud, lay along the ground, one foot hooked over the other. Her whole air was one of languor and concentration. To her father's "Hullo," she answered only in a faint muffled voice, "Hullo, Daddy."

"Hullo, Kate." But he said no more and did not go near. Quick never asked for affection from his girls. He despised fathers who flirted with their daughters, who encouraged them to love. It would have been especially wrong, he thought, with these two. They were naturally impulsive and affectionate— Jenny had moods of passionate devotion, especially in the last months. She was growing up, he thought, more quickly than Kate, and she was going to be an exciting woman, strong in all her feelings, intelligent, reflective. "Well, Jenny," he said, "what are you reading now?" But the child answered only by a slight wriggle of her behind.

Quick was amused at his own disappointment. He said to himself, "Children have no manners but at least they're honest —they never pretend." He fetched himself a deck chair and the morning paper, which he had hardly looked at before his early start on the road. He would make the best of things. At fifty-two, having lost most of his illusions, he was good at making the best of things. "It's a lovely day," he thought, "and I'm free till Sunday night." He looked round him as he opened the paper and felt again the pleasure of the garden. What a joy, at last, to be at peace. And the mere presence of the children was a pleasure. Nothing could deprive him of that. He was home again.

Jenny had got up and wandered away among the trees; her legs too were bare and dirty, and her dress had a large green stain at the side. She had been in the pond. And now Kate allowed herself to collapse slowly out of the swing and lay on her back with her hair tousled in the dirt, her arms thrown apart, her small dirty hands with black nails turned palm upwards to the sky. Her cocker bitch, Snort, came loping and sniffing, uttered one short bark and rooted at her mistress's legs. Kate raised one foot and tickled her stomach, then rolled over and buried her face in her arms. When Snort tried to push her nose under Kate's thigh as if to turn her over, she made a half kick and murmured, "Go away, Snort."

"Stop it, Snort," Jenny echoed in the same meditative tone. The sisters adored each other and one always came to the other's help. But Snort only stopped a moment to gaze at Jenny, then tugged at Kate's dress. Kate made another more energetic kick and said, "Oh, do go away, Snort."

Jenny stopped in her languid stroll, snatched a bamboo from the border, and hurled it at Snort like a spear.

The bitch, startled, uttered a loud uncertain bark and approached, wagging her behind so vigorously that she curled her body sideways at each wag. She was not sure if this was a new game, or if she had committed some grave crime. Jenny gave a yell and rushed at her. She fled yelping. At once Kate jumped up, seized another bamboo and threw it, shouting, "Tiger, tiger."

The two children dashed after the bitch, laughing, bumping together, falling over each other and snatching up anything they could find to throw at the fugitive, pebbles, dead daffodils, bits of flower-pots, lumps of earth. Snort, horrified, overwhelmed, dodged to and fro, barked hysterically, crazily, wagged her tail in desperate submission; finally put it between her legs and crept whining between a broken shed and the wall.

Robert was shocked. He was fond of the sentimental foolish Snort, and he saw her acute misery. He called to the children urgently, "Hi, Jenny—don't do that. Don't do that, Kate. She's frightened—you might put her eye out. Hi, stop—stop."

This last cry expressed real indignation. Jenny had got hold of a rake and was trying to hook Snort by the collar. Robert began to struggle out of his chair. But suddenly Kate turned round, aimed a pea-stick at him and shouted at the top of her voice, "Yield, Paleface." Jenny at once turned and cried, "Yes, yes—Paleface, yield." She burst into a shout of laughter and could not speak, but rushed at the man with the rake carried like a lance.

The two girls, staggering with laughter, threw themselves upon their father. "Paleface—Paleface Robbie. Kill him—scalp him. Torture him."

They tore at the man and suddenly he was frightened. It seemed to him that both the children, usually so gentle, so affectionate, had gone completely mad, vindictive. They were hurting him, and he did not know how to defend himself without hurting them, without breaking their skinny bones, which seemed as fragile as a bird's legs. He dared not even push too hard against the thin ribs which seemed to bend under his hand. Snort, suddenly recovering confidence, rushed barking from cover and seized this new victim by the sleeve, grunting and tugging.

"Hi," he shouted, trying to catch at the bitch. "Call her off, Kate. Don't, don't, children." But they battered at him, Kate was jumping on his stomach, Jenny had seized him by the collar as if to strangle him. Her face, close to his own, was that of a homicidal maniac; her eyes were wide and glaring, her lips were curled back to show all her teeth. And he was really strangling. He made a violent effort to throw the child off, but her hands were firmly twined in his collar. He felt his ears sing. Then suddenly the chair gave way—all three fell with a crash. Snort, startled, and perhaps pinched, gave a yelp, and snapped at the man's face.

Kate was lying across his legs, Jenny on his chest; she still held his collar in both hands. But now, gazing down at him, her expression changed. She cried, "Oh, she's bitten you. Look, Kate." Kate, rolling off his legs, came to her knees. "So she has, bad Snort."

The girls were still panting, flushed, struggling with laughter. But Jenny reproached her sister, "It's not a joke. It might be poisoned."

"I know," Kate was indignant. But burst out again into helpless giggles.

Robert picked himself up and dusted his coat. He did not utter any reproaches. He avoided even looking at the girls in case they should see his anger and surprise. He was deeply shocked. He could not forget Jenny's face, crazy, murderous; he thought, "Not much affection there—she wanted to hurt. It was as if she hated me."

It seemed to him that something new had broken into his old simple and happy relation with his daughters; that they had suddenly receded from him into a world of their own in which he had no standing, a primitive, brutal world.

He straightened his tie. Kate had disappeared; Jenny was gazing at his forehead and trying to suppress her own giggles. But when he turned away, she caught his arm, "Oh Daddy, where are you going?"

"To meet your mother—she must be on her way."

"Oh, but you can't go like that—we've got to wash your bite."

"That's all right, Jenny. It doesn't matter."

"But Kate is getting the water—and it might be quite bad."

And now, Kate, coming from the kitchen with a bowl of water, called out indignantly, "Sit down, Daddy—sit down—how dare you get up."

She was playing the stern nurse. And in fact, Robert, though still in a mood of disgust, found himself obliged to submit to this new game. At least it was more like a game. It was not murderous. And a man so plump and bald could not allow himself even to appear upset by the roughness of children. Even though the children would not understand why he was upset, why he was shocked.

"Sit down at once, man," Jenny said. "Kate, put up the chair."

Kate put up the chair, the two girls made him sit down, washed the cut, painted it with iodine, stuck a piece of plaster on it. Mrs. Quick, handsome, rosy, good-natured, practical, arrived in the middle of this ceremony, with her friend Jane Martin, Chairman of the Welfare Committee. Both were much amused by the scene, and the history of the afternoon. Their air said plainly to Robert, "All you children—amusing yourselves while we run the world."

Kate and Jenny were sent to wash and change their dirty frocks. The committee was coming to tea. And at tea, the two girls, dressed in smart clean frocks, handed round cake and bread and butter with demure and reserved looks. They knew how to behave at tea, at a party. They were enjoying the dignity of their own performance. Their eyes passed over their father as if he did not exist, or rather as if he existed only as another guest, to be waited on.

And now, seeking as it were a new if lower level of security, of resignation, he said to himself, "Heavens, but what did I expect? In a year or two more I shan't count at all. Young men will come prowling, like the dogs after Snort—I shall be an old buffer, useful only to pay bills."

The ladies were talking together about a case—the case of a

105

boy of fourteen, a nice respectable boy, most regular at Sunday school, who had suddenly robbed his mother's till and gone off in a stolen car. Jenny, seated at her mother's feet, was listening intently, Kate was feeding chocolate roll to Snort, and tickling her chin.

Quick felt all at once a sense of stuffiness. He wanted urgently to get away, to escape. Yes, he needed some male society. He would go to the club. Probably no one would be there but the card-room crowd, and he could not bear cards. But he might find old Wilkins in the billiard room. Wilkins at seventy was a crashing, a dreary bore, who spent half his life at the club; who was always telling you how he had foreseen the slump, and how clever he was at investing his money. What good was money to old Wilkins? But, Quick thought, he could get up a game with Wilkins, pass an hour or two with him, till dinner-time, even dine with him. He could phone his wife. She would not mind. She rather like a free evening for her various accounts. And he need not go home till the children were in bed.

And when after tea, the committee members pulled out their agenda, he stole away. Suddenly, as he turned by the corner house, skirting its front garden wall, he heard running steps and a breathless call. He turned, it was Jenny. She arrived, panting, holding herself by the chest. "Oh, I couldn't catch you."

"What is it now, Jenny?"

"I wanted to look—at the cut."

Robert began to stoop. But she cried, "No, I'll get on the wall. Put me up."

He lifted her on the garden wall which made her about a foot taller than himself. Having reached this superior position, she poked the plaster.

"I just wanted to make sure it was sticking. Yes, it's all right."

She looked down at him with an expression he did not recognize. What was the game, medical, material? Was she going to laugh? But the child frowned. She was also struck by something new and unexpected.

Then she tossed back her hair. "Good-bye." She jumped down and ran off. The man walked slowly towards the club. "No," he thought, "not quite a game—not for half a second. She's growing up—and so am I."

Could such events have happened in your own family? Try to define for yourself the discoveries Robert Quick makes about his daughters and himself.

Does Quick seem to you a good parent, as they go?

Why does the writer introduce (A) *the tea-party with the Welfare Committee?* (B) *the story about the fourteen-year-old boy?* (C) *Wilkins?*

What is Quick's main reason for wanting to go to the club (there is a strong clue in one particular sentence)?

FOR FURTHER READING: William Golding. *Lord of the Flies*. (Faber School Editions.) This now famous book develops to their fullest extent the uncomfortable suggestions of the moment when Jenny nearly strangles her father. A number of schoolboys are stranded on a desert island; the way they react shows frighteningly certain truths not only about children, but about all mankind.

Compare *Growing Up* also with D. H. Lawrence's *Tickets, Please*, which occurs later in this book.

Joyce Cary wrote many books which you will enjoy reading soon, if not now. This story is from *Spring Song*, his collected short stories. Two particularly entertaining novels are *The Horse's Mouth*—about a socially unacceptable but very likeable painter—and *Charley Is My Darling*, a sympathetic account of how an able but unlucky boy becomes what society calls a "delinquent". These are published by Michael Joseph and Penguins.

T. F. POWYS

Powys is like no other writer in this book, or possibly in English; he is sometimes compared to John Bunyan, but for most of us today he is a good deal more readable. He was a countryman, in whom the best traditions of rural life lived on; and there is almost nothing modern about his writing. He is never far from the fable, or allegory—a story standing for much more than its surface tale; behind Powys's countrymen are the biggest abstractions: good, evil, death, God, and above all love. And he treats this difficult material humbly, with a quiet humour.

Fundamentally Powys is a serious writer; and when he seems to be a simpleton, he is perhaps most wise. A full understanding of *Lie Thee Down, Oddity!* is possibly beyond any of us; but I hope you will like it and want to think it over.

Lie Thee Down, Oddity!

Though the sun shone with summer heat, the damp August warmth giving the rather faded countryside a new glow in her cheeks—for there had been a good all-night's rain—yet Mr. Cronch wore his black felt hat, of the cut that used to be worn by evangelical clergymen in the last century.

The Honourable George Bullman, who employed Mr.

Cronch as head-gardener, had spoken to him some years before about this hat of his, which was the only thing about Mr. Cronch that gave a hint of peculiarities. "Your Methodist hat will be the ruin of you one day, Cronch," Mr. Bullman had observed, while discussing with his gardener the making of a new lawn.

Mr. Cronch was mowing the lawn; he had bid the under-gardener work elsewhere. To please and humour Cronch, Mr. Bullman used no motor-mowing machine. Cronch did not like them. But the under-gardener had hardly looked at the old-fashioned mower before he complained that such labour was beyond his power. To push all day such an awkward instrument "that might", the young man said, "have been used by Adam" was out of the question for anyone who understood the arts and fancies of oil-driven machinery.

Mr. Cronch did the work himself. "One has, you know, to pay for one's oddities," he told his wife Jane.

At Green Gate House the grounds were always in the best order; there was never a weed in the kitchen-garden or a plantain on the lawn, but in one place, bordering the lawn, there were railings, and over these railings there was the heath.

A different world, that looked with contempt upon the soft pelt of a smooth lawn, which was indeed like the skin of a tamed beast that did nothing else but lie and bask in the sun while its sleek hide was being curry-combed by Mr. Cronch. The heath was a different matter from the garden. All was nature there, and she is a wild, fierce, untutored mother. Flowers and weeds, unnoticed, lived there, fighting the battle of their lives, careless of man, but living as they were commanded to live at the first moving of the waters. The raven and the falcon nested in the tall trees beyond a desolate swamp, and only a solitary heath-cutter might sometimes be seen with his load, taking a long track towards the waste land. Who, indeed, would view such barrenness when there was the Honourable George Bullman's garden to admire?

Mr. Bullman could afford a good gardener. The head-gardener's cottage, where Mr. Cronch and his wife lived, had every comfort of a modern well-built house. No servant of Mr. Bullman had anything to complain of. No one would leave such service, could they avoid doing so.

Over the heath, even the winds blew differently from the gentle garden ones. Out there the blasts could roar and bellow, wrench the boughs from the trees, and rush along madly, but in the summer-time garden all winds were soft.

Mr. Cronch stopped. He took the box from the mower and tipped the cut grass into the wheelbarrow. The wheelbarrow was full of sweet-smelling grass. Mr. Cronch then whistled softly, and Robert, the under-gardener, left his weeding and trundled the barrow to the cucumber-frames. He returned with the empty barrow at a slow, even pace—the gait of a well-paid gardener, as learned from Mr. Cronch.

Mr. Cronch began to mow again. He came near to the railings beyond which was the heath. Then he stopped. He took off his hat and looked into it. He looked at the lawn. Nowhere in the world, out of England, could any lawn have been smoother or more green. There was not the smallest clover leaf there that was not consecrated to the fine taste of a proper gentleman, and ready to be pressed by the elegant foot of a real lady. The smooth banks, the beds of flowers near by, might have been a modern picture in colours; they were so unlike nature. There was nothing rude or untidy there, and every cabbage in the kitchen-garden wore a coronet.

Mr. Cronch should, after a little rest, have continued to push the machine, but instead of doing so, he looked over the railings at the heath.

Mr. Cronch had not changed, as the garden was changed when it became the heath. He was the same Mr. Cronch who had, at one o'clock, cut the finest cucumber in the garden for

Mr. Bullman's lunch. He waited for another moment or two and then softly put on his hat. After doing so, he spoke aloud. "Lie thee down, Oddity!" said Mr. Cronch.

Then Mr. Cronch shook his head, as much as to say that if the Oddity would not lie down, it was no fault of his. For such a being it was impossible to control. Had the Oddity lain down, then Mr. Cronch would have gone on with his work, as a wise man should, who earns four pounds a week, with a good house and garden, and with leave to sell whatever he likes from his master's.

But Mr. Cronch did not start work again. It was no good; whatever happened to him the Oddity must be obeyed. The Oddity knew best. Mr. Cronch left the machine where it was, near to the railings. He walked with the same slow gardener's walk—that showed, as much as any walk could, a hatred of all untidiness and disorder—and came to the potting-shed. Then he put on his coat.

The hour was three in the afternoon. Mr. Cronch learned that from his watch. Then he listened. What he expected, happened; the church clock that was just across the way struck three.

Mr. Cronch's watch was always right.

It was no use mentioning that to the Oddity. He would not lie down the more because Mr. Cronch's gold watch—a gift of Mr. Bullman's—went with the church time.

Mr. Cronch shut the potting-shed door and went home. He remarked, when he saw his wife, as though he said nothing of particular interest, that he had given up work at Green Gate House. He told her to begin to pack, for they were leaving the gardener's cottage as soon as possible.

Jane thought him mad, and when the under-gardener, Robert, heard of it, he blamed the mowing-machine. "To have to push anything like that would drive any man away," he said to Mr. Bullman.

The Honourable George Bullman was anxious that Mr. Cronch should still remain in the gardener's cottage. He would give him a pension, he said, for he did not want to lose so good a neighbour, whose advice he valued so highly. Mr. Bullman, of course, blamed the hat for the trouble.

Jane wished to stay, but as the Oddity would not lie down, Mr. Cronch said they must go.

About two miles away from Green Gate House, upon the heath, there was a wretched cottage that had once been inhabited by a rabbit-catcher. Mr. Cronch chose this hut as a residence. About an acre of land went with it. Mr. Cronch repaired the cottage with his own hands, and put up new railings round the garden. In order to do this neatly he spent most of the money he had saved in service. Then he began to reclaim the garden, that was fallen out of cultivation and had become heath again.

The wild spirit of the waste land struggled against him. But here the poverty of the soil met its match. Nature is no respecter of persons; she gives alike to the good and to the evil. The potato-blight will ruin a good man's crop as well as a naughty one's. The heath was not a curry-combed creature, tamed with milk and wine. It was a savage animal, now friendly and kind, now cruel and vindictive, then mild. One day smiling like a pretty maid, and the next biting at you with ugly-shaped teeth.

There was no pleasant shelter there, no glass-houses. No high walls, no trimmed box-hedges. The winds of Heaven had free passage, a snake could roam at large and find only its natural enemies to attack it. The wild birds had rest. Mr. Cronch bowed his head and laboured. It needed something stronger than nature to cast him down. With the Oddity asleep, he could go on with his work. There was no need for him to rest, he was an obedient servant. He required no telling what to do in the way of work; even the Honourable

George Bullman had put himself under Mr. Cronch's guidance. While he had hands and tools he could compel the most sour-tempered soil to serve his needs. His broad shoulders were ever bent over the ground as he turned the earthen clod.

It was not long before Mr. Cronch compelled the heath to pay him tribute, and soon a pleasant cottage and a large well-cultivated garden arose in the wilderness. There were many who respected Mr. Cronch for leaving so much good at Mr. Bullman's to do battle with nature upon the heath, but others said he only left his master out of pride. Mr. Cronch smiled when he heard that. "Here was a fine matter, indeed," he thought, "that a mortal man should have pride—a nice folly to call a leaf proud that is driven willy-nilly before a November gale. A fine pride that leaf must have when, at the last, it is buried in a dunghill!"

But if Mr. Cronch was proud, as some thought, it was only because he had the knowledge that, within him, something slept. . . .

Mr. Cronch was resting contentedly one Sunday, reading a country paper. Even that morning he had been busy in his garden, and was glad now to rest while Jane prepared the dinner.

Mr. Cronch sat there, a simple, working-class man, respectable—in years too—wearing spectacles, and reading his paper.

He found something to read that interested him, for he read the same paragraph three times.

This was a police case. An old woman, who was employed on Saturdays by the Stonebridge town clerk to scrub his floors, had found upon the dining-room floor a blank cheque. This cheque she had filled in herself, and because she was a simple woman, without pride, she had written the town clerk's name instead of her own.

For thirty years Mrs. Tibby had kept herself and her husband John—who spent all his time in leaning over the town bridge to watch the water flow under—and now his one wish was to go to London to see the King. His wife wished to give him this treat. "'E do need a holiday," she said.

When a charwoman picks up money she has a right to it. Mrs. Tibby thought the cheque money. Money, after a card-party, which there had been at the clerk's, is often left on the floor for the sweeper—that is the custom of the country.

Mrs. Tibby was not greedy; she only wrote "four pounds" upon the cheque. She supposed that sum to be enough to take her husband to see the King. If the clerk were annoyed, she knew she could work the money out in scrubbing the floors.

When she was taken up, she could get no bail, so she went to prison.

Mr. Cronch carefully folded the paper.

The month was November. Over the heath, dark sweeping clouds, like great besoms, were driving. The two ravens, who nested in the high fir tree, enjoyed the wind. The mist from the sea brought memories to their minds; they remembered stories told of men hanged in chains on Blacknoll Mound, whose bones could be pecked clean. The ravens flew off and looked for a lamb to kill.

Mr. Cronch laid the paper on the table, beside a smoking dish of fried beef and onions—there were other vegetables to come—and a rice pudding.

Mr. Cronch rose slowly and sniffed.

But the Oddity would not lie down. So Mr. Cronch told his wife he was going out. The distance to Stonebridge was twelve miles. Mr. Cronch put on his overcoat; he went to a drawer and took out twenty-five pounds. He put on his large black hat, opened the cottage-door and went out—the rain greeted him with a lively shower of water-drops. Jane let him go. She supposed him to be in one of his mad fits, that the Giant Despair in the *Pilgrim's Progress* used to have.

Mr. Cronch walked along with his usual slow, steady step—

the gait of a careful gardener. When he reached Stonebridge he was not admitted into the jail, and so he took a lodging for the night.

In the morning he visited Mrs. Tibby. "I wish to be your bail," he said cheerfully.

Mrs. Tibby was in a maze. She did not know what she had done wrong. She was happy where she was, she was allowed to gossip with the prison charwoman, who was an old friend of hers. She begged Mr. Cronch, if he wished to be good to her, to allow her to stay with her friend, and to take her husband to London to see the King. Mrs. Tibby liked the prison. "Everyone is so kind," she said, "and when I complained to the doctor about my headaches, he ordered me gin. I have never been so happy before."

Mr. Cronch found Mr. Tibby smoking his pipe and leaning over the town bridge. He told him he was going to take him to see the King, and Mr. Tibby agreed to go, but first he knocked out his pipe on the stone coping of the bridge.

When they reached London, the King was out of town. He was soon to return, and Mr. Tibby spent the time happily, smoking his pipe and leaning over Waterloo Bridge, although the fog was so dense he could not see the river. When the King came, Mr. Cronch took Mr. Tibby into the crowd to see the King go by. Mr. Tibby sang "God Save the King", and shouted "Hurrah!" The King bowed.

"Now I shall die happy," said Mr. Tibby, "but how shall I get home?"

Mr. Cronch paid his fare to Stonebridge, and saw him off at the station.

The weather had improved; a brisk wind from the southwest had driven off the fog. Mr. Cronch, to please himself, walked into the city. He had fifteen pounds in his pocket, and he looked into the shop windows. He still wore his large black hat and the beggars avoided him. They thought him a Jewish money-lender, or else a Baptist minister. Beggars are shrewd judges of character. They have to decide quickly. Their income depends upon it. To beg from the wrong man means loss of time—perhaps prison.

Mr. Cronch went down a narrow street where some offices were. One of these was the office of a money-lender. A gentleman, who looked worn out by sickness and trouble, came out of the door. A woman, his wife, who carried a baby in her arms, waited for him in the street. The gentleman shook his head. Evidently the security that he had to offer was not good enough.

Then there arose a little conversation between them.

"I could go to mother's," the woman said.

"If I had money, I could go with you," the man observed, "the change would do me good, and I might get work in Bristol."

"Baby will be easier to manage in a few months," the woman said. "Mother will not mind taking us, but you will have to stay here."

"I can't let you go," said the man.

He made a curious sound in his throat.

Mr. Cronch stood near on the pavement. Who would have noticed Mr. Cronch? The couple paid no heed to him. But presently they turned to where he stood, for Mr. Cronch spoke.

"Lie thee down, Oddity!" he said aloud.

The gentleman smiled, he could do nothing else. The baby held out her arms to Mr. Cronch; she wanted his hat. Mr. Cronch took two five-pound notes from his wallet and gave them to the woman. Then he walked away.

For his own pleasure, he walked out of the city into the poor parts of the town. He walked along slowly and looked at the vegetables in the greengrocers' shops. He wondered that people could buy such old stuff. If he offered anything like that at the Weyminster market, he would never find a purchaser. He remembered the lordly freedom of the wild heath. There, nature might be cruel, but life and death joined hands in the dance. The sun could shine, and when darkness came it was the darkness of God. The town was different.

Mr. Cronch went down a dingy court. Clothes were hung from house to house, and barefooted children played in the gutter. The air was heavy with human odours and factory stench. Then Mr. Cronch came upon something worse than misery.

A man sat leaning against a wall, with half his face eaten away. His eyes were gone; he cried out to everyone whose footstep he heard, to lead him to the river. When Mr. Cronch came by, he cried out the more. Mr. Cronch stopped.

"Lie thee down, Oddity!" he said angrily.

"Lead me to the river," the man begged.

"Come," said Mr. Cronch, and led the man to the river. A policeman, who knew the man's wish, followed them. At the brink of the river the man said, "I am afraid; only give me one little push, and I shall die."

"Certainly," said Mr. Cronch, and pushed him into the river. The man sank like a stone.

The police officer came up to demand Mr. Cronch's name and address; he had made a note of what had happened.

"You will appear at court, charged with murder," he said. "But now you may go!"

Mr. Cronch walked out of the great city. He had enough money to take him home by train, but he liked walking. As he went along he decided to plant a part of his garden with spinach. He had seen a good deal of this green stuff in the London shops, and he thought he could sell it at home.

He walked ten miles out of town, and then took a lodging for the night. Since the Oddity had risen last, Mr. Cronch had behaved just as a sober gardener would when out for a holiday.

When he came to an allotment he would look into it to see what was grown. He found the ground good. But he believed that more glass might be used, and the city dung he thought too heating for the soil. He was especially interested in the window-flowers that he saw, but wondered that no hyacinths were seen, the bulbs having been all planted too late to bloom at that season.

Starting his walk again the next morning, Mr. Cronch came upon a large crowd watching a high factory chimney. This immense chimney, as high as the clouds and weighing many hundreds of tons, was being brought down. The workmen were busy at its base, and the crowd watched from a safe distance.

All was ready for the fall; the masons and engineers left the chimney. But one of the men remained to give the final stroke that would cause the huge structure to sway and fall. This mason completed his task, and began to walk to safety.

When he was a few yards off the chimney, he trod upon a wet plank hidden in the mud, and fell heavily. The spectators expected him to jump up and run off. But he did not do so.

An official held his watch in his hand, "One, two, three," he counted. When he reached sixty seconds the chimney would fall.

Its direction was known. It would fall directly upon the man. He tried to rise, but his leg was broken. He tried to crawl, but the pain prevented him. He raised himself up, and looked at the huge mass above him; he knew what was coming. None of the onlookers moved. It was too late to save the man; to go to him would mean certain death.

The chimney began to totter, to rock.

Then Mr. Cronch said softly, "Lie thee down, Oddity!" but the Oddity would not listen to him. Mr. Cronch spoke in so low a tone that perhaps the Oddity never even heard what he said.

Mr. Cronch walked with his slow gardener's step, to the man.

"What are you afraid of?" he asked him.

"Of the chimney," cried the man, "it's falling."

"What if it does fall," observed Mr. Cronch, looking up as though he thought the huge mass above him was a small pear tree.

"It's coming," cried the man.

Mr. Cronch took off his hat. The man smiled.

Mr. Cronch is not a clergyman; the writer emphasizes frequently that he is simply a good gardener (and what, he implies, is better than that?). Yet the hat is clearly associated with the "oddity" of saintliness (though this is a wishy-washy word for Mr. Cronch's robust goodness). Notice how the baby is attracted to it, and how it gives strength and courage finally to the man about to be crushed by the chimney.

Why, near the beginning, does Powys quote the under-gardener's words about Adam? Would Mr. Cronch be annoyed by this remark?

Powys chooses his words carefully in contrasting the rich man's garden and the wild heath. Study how he gradually makes his own preference clear.

There are people like Mr. Cronch in the world. Most people congratulate themselves if they can work a beautiful garden well, and keep their watches in time with the church (what does this really imply?). But a few great ones, with this Oddity, are not content with that; and they voluntarily leave the easy situation, to tackle something more difficult and more urgent. And sometimes, like Mr. Cronch with the policeman, and like Christ with the Pharisees, they come up against worldly authority as they do so. Whom do you know of who might fit

Mr. Cronch's hat? Be careful—notice that above all Mr. Cronch is not proud *of his own achievement, and seeks no glory for himself.*

FOR FURTHER READING: *God's Eyes A-Twinkle*—stories of T. F. Powys. Chatto and Windus.

PATRICK O'BRIAN

Besides the book of short stories from which *Samphire* is taken, Patrick O'Brian has published several novels; and he has also written for children. This tale, in many ways horrific, is told with a glassy calm which I find remarkable.

Samphire

Sheer, sheer, the white cliff rising, straight up from the sea, so far that the riding waves were nothing but ripples on a huge calm. Up there, unless you leaned over, you did not see them break, but for all the distance the thunder of the water came loud. The wind, too, tearing in from the sea, rushing from a clear, high sky, brought the salt tang of the spray on their lips.

They were two, standing up there on the very edge of the cliff: they had left the levelled path and come down to the break itself and the man was crouched, leaning over as far as he dared.

"It *is* a clump of samphire, Molly," he said; then louder, half turning, "Molly, it *is* samphire. I *said* it was samphire, didn't I?" He had a high, rather unmasculine voice, and he emphasized his words.

His wife did not reply, although she had heard him the first time. The round of her chin was trembling like a child's before

122

it cries: there was something in her throat so strong that she could not have spoken it if it had been for her life.

She stepped a little closer, feeling cautiously for a firm foothold, and she was right on him and she caught the smell of his hairy tweed jacket. He straightened so suddenly that he brushed against her. "Hey, look out," he said, "I almost trod on your foot. Yes, it *was* samphire. I said so as soon as I saw it from down there. Have a look."

She could not answer, so she knelt and crawled to the edge. Heights terrified her, always had. She could not close her eyes; that only made it worse. She stared unseeing, while the brilliant air and the sea and the noise of the sea assaulted her terrified mind and she clung insanely to the thin grass. Three times he pointed it out, and the third time she heard him so as to be able to understand his words. ". . . fleshy leaves. You see the fleshy leaves? They used them for pickles. Samphire pickles!" He laughed, excited by the wind, and put his hand on her shoulder. Even then she writhed away, covering it by getting up and returning to the path.

He followed her. "You noted the *fleshy leaves*, didn't you, Molly? They allow the plant to store its nourishment. Like a cactus. Our *native* cactus. I *said* it was samphire at once, didn't I, although I have never actually seen it before. We could almost get it with a stick."

He was pleased with her for having looked over, and said that she was coming along very well: she remembered—didn't she?—how he had had to persuade her and persuade her to come up even the smallest cliff at first, how he had even to be a little firm. And now there she was going up the highest of them all, as bold as brass; and it was quite a dangerous cliff too, he said, with a keen glance out to sea, jutting his chin; but there she was as bold as brass looking over the top of it. He had been quite right insisting, hadn't he? It was worth it when you were there, wasn't it? Between these questions he waited for a reply, a "yes" or hum of agreement. If he had not insisted she would always have stayed down there on the beach, wouldn't she? Like a lazy puss. He said, wagging his finger to show that he was not quite in earnest, that she should always listen to her Lacey (this was a pet name that he had coined for himself). Lacey was her lord and master, wasn't he? Love, honour, and obey?

He put his arm round her when they came to a sheltered turn of the path and began to fondle her, whispering in his secret night-voice, Tss-tss-tss, but he dropped her at once when some coast-guards appeared.

As they passed he said, "Good day, men," and wanted to stop to ask them what they were doing but they walked quickly on.

In the morning she said she would like to see the samphire again. He was very pleased and told the hotel-keeper that she was becoming quite the little botanist. He had already told him and the nice couple from Letchworth (they were called Jones and had a greedy daughter: he was an influential solicitor, and Molly would be a clever girl to be nice to them), he had already told them about the samphire, and he had said how he had recognized it at once from lower down, where the path turned, although he had only seen specimens in a *hortus siccus* and illustrations in books.

On the way he stopped at the tobacconist on the promenade to buy a stick. He was in high spirits. He told the man at once that he did not smoke, and made a joke about the shop being a house of ill-*fume*; but the tobacconist did not understand. He looked at the sticks that were in the shop but he did not find one for his money and they went out. At the next tobacconist, by the pier, he made the same joke to the man there. She stood near the door, not looking at anything. In the end he paid the marked price for an ash walking-stick with a crook, though at first he had proposed a shilling less: he told the man that they were not ordinary summer people, because they were going to have a villa there.

Walking along past the pier towards the cliff path, he put the stick on his shoulder with a comical gesture, and when they came to the car park where a great many people were coming down to the beach with picnics and pneumatic rubber toys he sang, We are the boys that nothing can tire; we are the boys that gather samphire. When a man who was staying in the same hotel passed near them, he called out that they were going to see if they could get a bunch of jolly good samphire that they had seen on the cliff yesterday. The man nodded.

It was a long way to the highest cliff, and he fell silent for a little while. When they began to climb he said that he would never go out without a stick again; it was a fine, honest thing, an ashplant, and a great help. Didn't she think it was a great help? Had she noticed how he had chosen the best one in the shop, and really it was very cheap, though perhaps they had better go without tea tomorrow to make it up. She remembered, didn't she, what they had agreed after their discussion about an exact allowance for every day? He was walking a few feet ahead of her, so that each time he had to turn his head for her answer.

It was blowing harder than the day before on the top, and for the last hundred yards he kept silent, or at least she did not hear him say anything.

At the turn of the path he cried, "It is still there. Oh jolly good. It is still there, Molly," and he pointed out how he had first seen the samphire, and repeated, shouting over the wind, that he had been sure of it at once.

For a moment she looked at him curiously while he stared over and up where the plant grew on the face of the cliff, the wind ruffling the thin, fluffy hair that covered his baldness, and a keen expression on his face; and for a moment she wondered whether it was perhaps possible that he saw beauty there. But the moment was past and the voice took up again its unceasing dumb cry: Go on, oh, go on, for Christ's sake go on, go on, go on, oh go *on*.

They were there. He had made her look over. "Note the fleshy leaves," he had said; and he had said something about samphire pickle! and how the people at the hotel would stare when they brought it back. That was just before he began to crouch over, turned from her so that his voice was lost.

He was leaning right over. It was quite true when he said that he had no fear of heights: once he had astonished the workmen on the steeple of her uncle's church by walking among the scaffolding and planks with all the aplomb of a steeplejack. He was reaching down with his left arm, his right leg doubled under him and his right arm extended on the grass: his other leg was stretched out along the break of the cliff.

Once again there was the strong grip in her throat; her stomach was rigid and she could not keep her lip from trembling. She could hardly see, but as he began to get up her eyes focused. She was already there, close on him—she had never gone back to the path this time. God give me strength, but as she pushed him she felt her arms weak like jelly.

Instantly his face turned; absurd, baby-face surprise and a shout unworded. The extreme of horror on it, too. He had been half up when she thrust at him, with his knee off the ground, the stick hand over and the other clear of the grass. He rose, swaying out. For a second the wind bore his body and the stick scrabbled furiously for a purchase on the cliff. There where the samphire grew, a little above, it found a hard ledge, gripped. Motionless in equilibrium for one timeless space—a cinema stopped in action—then his right hand gripped the soil, tore, ripped the grass and he was up, from the edge, crouched, gasping huge sobbing draughts of air on the path.

He was screaming at her in an agonized falsetto interrupted by painful gasps, searching for air and life. "You pushed me, Molly you—pushed me. You—pushed me."

She stood silent, looking down and the voice rushed over her. You pushed—you pushed me—Molly. She found she could swallow again, and the hammering in her throat was less. By now his voice had dropped an octave: he had been speaking without a pause but for his gasping—the gasping had stopped now, and he was sitting there normally. ". . . not well; a spasm. Wasn't it, Molly?" he was saying; and she heard him say "accident" sometimes.

Still she stood, stone-still and grey and later he was saying ". . . *possibly* live together? How can we *possibly* look at one another? After this?" And some time after it seemed to her that he had been saying something about their having taken their room for the month . . . accident was the word, and spasm, and not well—fainting? It was, wasn't it, Molly? There was an unheard note in his voice.

She turned and began to walk down the path. He followed at once. By her side he was, and his face was turned to hers, peering into her face, closed face. His visage, his whole face, everything, had fallen to pieces: she looked at it momentarily —a very old terribly frightened comforting-itself small child. He had fallen off a cliff all right.

He touched her arm, still speaking, pleading. "It *was* that, wasn't it, Molly? You didn't push me, Molly. It was an accident. . . ."

She turned her dying face to the ground, and there were her feet marching on the path; one, the other; one, the other; down, down, down.

Samphire is referred to in KING LEAR as growing on Dover Cliff, and "Lacey" (of course) is correct in his account of it.

At the moment of the push he shows "baby-face surprise". Does this adjective support any impression you have formed earlier?

Decide for yourself what the writer means, at the end, by "He had fallen off a cliff all right" and "her dying face".

We never learn Molly's husband's real name (and you will have your own feelings about his choosing "a pet-name for himself"); this story leaves much of the background to our guesswork, though the special incidents are described in sharp detail. It seems to me that page 125 suggests that the couple are on their honeymoon, which would make the story still more horrifying. Do you agree?

This is a disagreeable story; the husband, in a realistic way, is quite insufferable, and yet Molly cannot escape. If you like it, as I do, try to explain your liking to yourself.

D. H. LAWRENCE

Lawrence was born in 1885, the son of a miner, and by brilliance as a scholar, as a writer, and as a person quickly rose to enter, and then tower above, the artistic world of the First World War and the years following. Before his death in 1930, Lawrence and his wife travelled widely; but this story is set in his home region of Nottinghamshire, during the war. It is in some respects more humorous, in some more horrifying, than most of Lawrence's work; but the vitality, the warmth, and the honesty about human relationships are all here, and are typical of the man.

Tickets, Please

There is in the Midlands a single-line tramway system which boldly leaves the county town and plunges off into the black, industrial countryside, up hill and down dale, through the long ugly villages of workmen's houses, over canals and railways, past churches perched high and noble over the smoke and shadows, through stark, grimy cold little market-places, tilting away in a rush past cinemas and shops down to the hollow where the collieries are, then up again, past a little rural church, under the ash trees, on in a rush to the terminus, the last little ugly place of industry, the cold little town that shivers on the edge of the wild, gloomy country beyond. There the green and creamy coloured tram-cars seem to pause and purr with curious satisfaction. But in a few minutes—the clock on the turret of the Co-operative Wholesale Society's shops gives the time—away it starts once more on the adventure. Again there are the reckless swoops downhill, bouncing the loops: again the chilly wait in the hill-top market-place: again the breathless slithering round the precipitous drop under the church: again the patient halts at the loops, waiting for the oncoming car: so on and on, for two long hours, till at last the city looms beyond the fat gas-works, the narrow factories draw near, we are in the sordid streets of the great town, once more we sidle to a standstill at our terminus, abashed by the great crimson and cream-coloured city cars, but still perky, jaunty, somewhat dare-devil, green as a jaunty sprig of parsley out of a black colliery garden.

To ride on these cars is always an adventure. Since we are in war-time, the drivers are men unfit for active service: cripples and hunchbacks. So they have the spirit of the devil in them. The ride becomes a steeplechase. Hurray! we have leapt in a clear jump over the canal bridge—now for the four-lane corner. With a shriek and a trail of sparks we are clear again. To be sure, a tram often leaps the rails—but what matter! It sits still in a ditch until other trams come to haul it out. It is quite common for a car, packed with one solid mass of living people, to come to a dead halt in the midst of unbroken blackness, the heart of nowhere on a dark night, and for the driver and the girl conductor to call: "All get off— car's on fire!" Instead, however, of rushing out in a panic, the passengers stolidly reply: "Get on—get on! We're not coming out. We're stopping where we are. Push on, George." So till flames actually appear.

The reason for this reluctance to dismount is that the nights are howlingly cold, black, and windswept, and a car is a haven

130

of refuge. From village to village the miners travel, for a change of cinema, of girl, of pub. The trams are desperately packed. Who is going to risk himself in the black gulf outside, to wait perhaps an hour for another tram, then to see the forlorn notice "Depot Only", because there is something wrong! Or to greet a unit of three bright cars all so tight with people that they sail past with a howl of derision. Trams that pass in the night.

This, the most dangerous tram-service in England, as the authorities themselves declare, with pride, is entirely conducted by girls, and driven by rash young men, a little crippled, or by delicate young men, who creep forward in terror. The girls are fearless young hussies. In their ugly blue uniform, skirts up to their knees, shapeless old peaked caps on their heads, they have all the sang-froid of an old non-commisioned officer. With a tram packed with howling colliers, roaring hymns downstairs and a sort of antiphony of obscenities upstairs, the lasses are perfectly at their ease. They pounce on the youths who try to evade their ticket-machine. They push off the men at the end of their distance. They are not going to be done in the eye—not they. They fear nobody —and everybody fears them.

"Hello, Annie!"

"Hello, Ted!"

"Oh, mind my corn, Miss Stone. It's my belief you've got a heart of stone, for you've trod on it again."

"You should keep it in your pocket," replied Miss Stone, and she goes sturdily upstairs in her high boots.

"Tickets, please."

She is peremptory, suspicious, and ready to hit first. She can hold her own against ten thousand. The step of that tram-car is her Thermopylae.

Therefore, there is a certain wild romance aboard these cars—and in the sturdy bosom of Annie herself. The time for

131

soft romance is in the morning, between ten o'clock and one, when things are rather slack: that is, except market-day and Saturday. Thus Annie has time to look about her. Then she often hops off her car and into a shop where she has spied something, while the driver chats in the main road. There is very good feeling between the girls and the drivers. Are they not companions in peril, shipments aboard this careering vessel of a tram-car, for ever rocking on the waves of a stormy land?

Then also, during the easy hours, the inspectors are most in evidence. For some reason, everybody employed in this tram-service is young: there are no grey heads. It would not do. Therefore the inspectors are of the right age, and one, the chief, is also good-looking. See him stand on a wet, gloomy morning, in his long oilskin, his peaked cap well down over his eyes, waiting to board a car. His face ruddy, his small brown moustache is weathered, he had a faint impudent smile. Fairly tall and agile, even in his waterproof, he springs aboard a car and greets Annie.

"Hello, Annie! Keeping the wet out?"

"Trying to."

There are only two people in the car. Inspecting is soon over. Then for a long and impudent chat on the foot-board, a good, easy, twelve-mile chat.

The inspector's name is John Thomas Raynor—always called John Thomas, except sometimes, in malice, Coddy. His face sets in fury when he is addressed, from a distance, with this abbreviation. There is considerable scandal about John Thomas in half a dozen villages. He flirts with the girl conductors in the morning, and walks out with them in the dark night, when they leave their tram-car at the depot. Of course, the girls quit the service frequently. Then he flirts and walks out with the newcomer: always providing she is sufficiently attractive, and that she will consent to walk. It is remarkable, however, that most of the girls are quite comely, they are all young, and this roving life aboard the car gives them a sailor's dash and recklessness. What matter how they behave when the ship is in port? Tomorrow they will be aboard again.

Annie, however, was something of a Tartar, and her sharp tongue had kept John Thomas at arm's length for many months. Perhaps, therefore, she liked him all the more; for he always came up smiling, with impudence. She watched him vanquish one girl, then another. She could tell by the movement of his mouth and eyes, when he flirted with her in the morning, that he had been walking out with this lass, or the other, the night before. A fine cock-of-the-walk he was. She could sum him up pretty well.

In this subtle antagonism they knew each other like old friends, they were as shrewd with one another almost as man and wife. But Annie had always kept him sufficiently at arm's length. Besides, she had a boy of her own.

The Statutes fair, however, came in November, at Bestwood. It happened that Annie had the Monday night off. It was a drizzling ugly night, yet she dressed herself up and went to the fair-ground. She was alone, but she expected soon to find a pal of some sort.

The roundabouts were veering round and grinding out their music, the side-shows were making as much commotion as possible. In the coconut shies there were no coconuts, but artificial wartime substitutes, which the lads declared were fastened into the irons. There was a sad decline in brilliance and luxury. None the less, the ground was muddy as ever, there was the same crush, the press of faces lighted up by the flares and the electric lights, the same smell of naphtha and a few potatoes, and of electricity.

Who should be the first to greet Miss Annie on the showground but John Thomas. He had a black overcoat buttoned up to his chin, and a tweed cap pulled down over his brows, his face between was ruddy and smiling and handy as ever. She knew so well the way his mouth moved.

She was very glad to have a "boy". To be at the Statutes without a fellow was no fun. Instantly, like the gallant he was, he took her on the Dragons, grim-toothed, roundabout switchbacks. It was not nearly so exciting as a tram-car actually. But, then, to be seated in a shaking, green dragon, uplifted above the sea of bubble faces, careering in a rickety fashion in the lower heavens, whilst John Thomas leaned over her, his cigarette in his mouth, was after all the right style. She was a plump, quick, alive little creature. So she was quite excited and happy.

John Thomas made her stay on for the next round. And therefore she could hardly for shame repulse him when he put his arm round her and drew her a little nearer to him, in a very warm and cuddly manner. Besides, he was fairly discreet, he kept his movement as hidden as possible. She looked down, and saw that his red, clean hand was out of sight of the crowd. And they knew each other so well. So they warmed up to the fair.

After the dragons they went on the horses. John Thomas paid each time, so she could but be complaisant. He, of course, set astride on the outer horse—named "Black Bess"—and she sat sideways, towards him, on the inner horse—named "Wildfire". But of course John Thomas was not going to sit discreetly on "Black Bess", holding the brass bar. Round they spun and heaved, in the light. And round he swung on his wooden steed, flinging one leg across her mount, and perilously tipping up and down, across the space, half lying back, laughing at her. He was perfectly happy; she was afraid her hat was on one side, but she was excited.

He threw quoits on a table, and won for her two large, pale blue hat-pins. And then, hearing the noise of the cinemas, announcing another performance, they climbed the boards and went in.

Of course, during these performances pitch darkness falls from time to time, when the machine goes wrong. Then there is a wild whooping, and a loud smacking of simulated kisses. In these moments John Thomas drew Annie towards him. After all, he had a wonderfully warm, cosy way of holding a girl with his arm, he seemed to make such a nice fit. And, after all, it was pleasant to be so held: so very comforting and cosy and nice. He leaned over her and she felt his breath on her hair; she knew he wanted to kiss her on the lips. And, after all, he was so warm and she fitted in to him so softly. After all, she wanted him to touch her lips.

But the light sprang up; she also started electrically, and put her hat straight. He left his arm lying nonchalantly behind her. Well, it was fun, it was exciting to be at the Statutes with John Thomas.

When the cinema was over they went for a walk across the dark, damp fields. He had all the arts of love-making. He was especially good at holding a girl, when he sat with her on a stile in the black, drizzling darkness. He seemed to be holding her in space, against his own warmth and gratification. And his kisses were soft and slow and searching.

So Annie walked out with John Thomas, though she kept her own body dangling in the distance. Some of the tram-girls chose to be huffy. But there, you must take things as you find them, in this life.

There was no mistake about it, Annie liked John Thomas a good deal. She felt so rich and warm in herself whenever he was near. And John Thomas really liked Annie, more than usual. The soft, melting way in which she could flow into a fellow, as if she melted into his very bones, was something rare and good. He fully appreciated this.

But with a developing acquaintance there began a develop-

135

ing intimacy. Annie wanted to consider him a person, a man; she wanted to take an intelligent interest in him, and to have an intelligent response. She did not want a mere nocturnal presence, which was what he was so far. And she prided herself that he could not leave her.

Here she made a mistake. John Thomas intended to remain a nocturnal presence; he had no idea of becoming an all-round individual to her. When she started to take an intelligent interest in him and his life and his character, he sheered off. He hated intelligent interest. And he knew that the only way to stop it was to avoid it. The possessive female was aroused in Annie. And so he left her.

It is no use saying she was not surprised. She was at first startled, thrown out of her count. For she had been so *very* sure of holding him. For a while she was staggered, and everything became uncertain to her. Then she wept with fury, indignation, desolation, and misery. Then she had a spasm of despair. And then, when he came, still impudently, on to her car, still familiar, but letting her see by the movement of his head that he had gone away to somebody else for the time being, and was enjoying pastures new, then she determined to have her own back.

She had a very shrewd idea what girls John Thomas had taken out. She went to Nora Purdy. Nora was a tall, rather pale, but well-built girl, with beautiful yellow hair. She was rather secretive.

"Hey!" said Annie, accosting her; then softly: "Who's John Thomas on with now?"

"I don't know," said Nora.

"Why, tha does," said Annie, ironically lapsing into dialect. "Tha knows as well as I do."

"Well, I do, then," said Nora. "It isn't me, so don't bother."

"It's Cissy Meakin, isn't it?"

"It is, for all I know."

"Hasn't he got a face on him?" said Annie. "I don't half like his cheek. I could knock him off the foot-board when he comes round at me."

"He'll get dropped on one of these days," said Nora.

"Ay, he will, when somebody makes up their mind to drop it on him. I should like to see him taken down a peg or two, shouldn't you?"

"I shouldn't mind," said Nora.

"You've got quite as much cause to as I have," said Annie. "But we'll drop on him one of these days, my girl. What? Don't you want to?"

"I don't mind," said Nora.

But as a matter of fact, Nora was much more vindictive than Annie.

One by one Annie went the round of the old flames. It so happened that Cissy Meakin left the tramway service in quite a short time. Her mother made her leave. Then John Thomas was on the qui vive. He cast his eyes over his old flock. And his eyes lighted on Annie. He thought she would be safe now. Besides, he liked her.

She arranged to walk home with him on Sunday night. It so happened that her car would be in the depot at half past nine: the last car would come in at 10.15. So John Thomas was to wait for her there.

At the depot the girls had a little waiting-room of their own. It was quite rough, but cosy, with a fire and an oven and a mirror, and table and wooden chairs. The half-dozen girls who knew John Thomas only too well had arranged to take service this Sunday afternoon. So, as the cars began to come in, early, the girls dropped into the waiting-room. And instead of hurrying off home, they sat around the fire and had a cup of tea. Outside was the darkness and lawlessness of wartime.

John Thomas came on the car after Annie, at about a

quarter to ten. He poked his head easily into the girls' waiting-room.

"Prayer-meeting?" he asked.

"Ay," said Laura Sharp. "Ladies only."

"That's me!" said John Thomas. It was one of his favourite exclamations.

"Shut the door, boy," said Muriel Baggaley.

"Oh, which side of me?" said John Thomas.

"Which tha likes," said Polly Birkin.

He had come in and closed the door behind him. The girls moved in their circle, to make a place for him near the fire. He took off his great-coat and pushed back his hat.

"Who handles the teapot?" he said.

Nora Purdy silently poured him out a cup of tea.

"Want a bit o' my bread and drippin'?" said Muriel Baggaley to him.

"Ay, give us a bit."

And he began to eat his piece of bread.

"There's no place like home, girls," he said.

They all looked at him as he uttered this piece of impudence. He seemed to be sunning himself in the presence of so many damsels.

"Especially if you're not afraid to go home in the dark," said Laura Sharp.

"Me! By myself I am."

They sat till they heard the last tram come in. In a few minutes Emma Houselay entered.

"Come on, my old duck!" cried Polly Birkin.

"It is perishing," said Emma, holding her fingers to the fire.

"But—I'm afraid to, go home in, the dark," sang Laura Sharp, the tune having got into her mind.

"Who're you going with tonight, John Thomas?" asked Muriel Baggaley coolly.

"Tonight?" said John Thomas. "Oh, I'm going home by myself tonight—all on my lonely-o."

"That's me!" said Nora Purdy, using his own ejaculation. The girls laughed shrilly.

"Me as well, Nora," said John Thomas.

"Don't know what you mean," said Laura.

"Yes, I'm toddling," said he, rising and reaching for his overcoat.

"Nay," said Polly. "We're all here waiting for you."

"We've got to be up in good time in the morning," he said, in the benevolent official manner.

They all laughed.

"Nay," said Muriel. "Don't leave us all lonely, John Thomas. Take one!"

"I'll take the lot, if you like," he responded gallantly.

"That you won't, either," said Muriel. "Two's company; seven's too much of a good thing."

"Nay—take one," said Laura. "Fair and square, all above board and say which."

"Ay," cried Annie, speaking for the first time. "Pick, John Thomas; let's hear thee."

"Nay," he said. "I'm going home quiet tonight. Feeling good, for once."

"Whereabouts?" said Annie. "Take a good 'un, then. But tha's got to take one of us!"

"Nay, how can I take one," he said, laughing uneasily. "I don't want to make enemies."

"You'd only make *one*," said Annie.

"The chosen *one*," added Laura.

"Oh, my! Who said girls!" exclaimed John Thomas, again turning, as if to escape. "Well—good night."

"Nay, you've got to make your pick," said Muriel. "Turn your face to the wall, and say which one touches you. Go on— we shall only just touch your back—one of us. Go on—turn your face to the wall, and don't look, and say which one touches you."

He was uneasy, mistrusting them. Yet he had not the courage to break away. They pushed him to a wall and stood him there with his face to it. Behind his back they all grimaced, tittering. He looked so comical. He looked around uneasily.

"Go on!" he cried.

"You're looking—you're looking!" they shouted.

He turned his head away. And suddenly, with a movement like a swift cat, Annie went forward and fetched him a box on the side of the head that sent his cap flying and himself staggering. He started round.

But at Annie's signal they all flew at him, slapping him, pinching him, pulling his hair, though more in fun than in spite or anger. He, however, saw red. His blue eyes flamed with strange fear as well as fury, and he butted through the girls to the door. It was locked. He wrenched at it. Roused, alert, the girls stood round and looked at him. He faced them, at bay. At that moment they were rather horrifying to him, as they stood in their short uniforms. He was distinctly afraid.

"Come on, John Thomas! Come on! Choose!" said Annie.

"What are you after? Open the door," he said.

"We shan't—not till you've chosen!" said Muriel.

"Chosen what?" he said.

"Chosen the one you're going to marry," she replied.

He hesitated a moment.

"Open the blasted door," he said, "and get back to your senses." He spoke with official authority.

"You've got to choose," cried the girls.

"Come on!" cried Annie, looking him in the eye. "Come on! Come on!"

He went forward, rather vaguely. She had taken off her belt, and swinging it, she fetched him a sharp blow over the head with the buckle end. He sprang and seized her. But

140

immediately the other girls rushed upon him, pulling and tearing and beating him. Their blood was now thoroughly up. He was their sport now. They were going to have their own back, out of him. Strange, wild creatures, they hung on him and rushed at him to bear him down. His tunic was torn right up the back, Nora had hold at the back of his collar, and was actually strangling him. Luckily the button burst. He struggled in a wild frenzy of fury and terror, almost mad terror. His tunic was simply torn off his back, his shirt-sleeves were torn away, his arms were naked. The girls rushed at him, clenched their hands on him and pulled at him: or they rushed at him and pushed him, butted him with all their might: or they struck him wild blows. He ducked and cringed and struck sideways. They became more intense.

At last he was down. They rushed on him, kneeling on him. He had neither breath nor strength to move. His face was bleeding with a long scratch, his brow was bruised.

Annie knelt on him, the other girls knelt and hung on to him. Their faces were flushed, their hair wild, their eyes were all glittering strangely. He lay at last quite still, with face averted, as an animal lies when it is defeated and at the mercy of the captor. Sometimes his eye glanced back at the wild faces of the girls. His breast rose heavily, his wrists were torn.

"Now, then, my fellow!" gasped Annie at length. "Now then—now——"

At the sound of her terrifying, cold triumph, he suddenly started to struggle as an animal might, but the girls threw themselves upon him with unnatural strength and power, forcing him down.

"Yes—now, then!" gasped Annie at length.

And there was a dead silence, in which the thud of heart-beating was to be heard. It was a suspense of pure silence in every soul.

"Now you know where you are," said Annie.

The sight of his white, bare arm maddened the girls. He lay in a kind of trance of fear and antagonism. They felt themselves filled with supernatural strength.

Suddenly Polly started to laugh—to giggle wildly—helplessly—and Emma and Muriel joined in. But Annie and Nora and Laura remained the same, tense, watchful, with gleaming eyes. He winced away from these eyes.

"Yes," said Annie, in a curious low tone, secret and deadly: "Yes! You've got it now. You know what you've done, don't you? You know what you've done."

He made no sound nor sign, but lay with bright, averted eyes and averted, bleeding face.

"You ought to be *killed*, that's what you ought," said Annie tensely. "You ought to be *killed*." And there was a terrifying lust in her voice.

Polly was ceasing to laugh, and giving long-drawn Oh-h-hs and sighs as she came to herself.

"He's got to choose," she said vaguely.

"Oh, yes, he has," said Laura, with vindictive decision.

"Do you hear—do you hear?" said Annie. And with a sharp movement, that made him wince, she turned his face to her.

"Do you hear?" she repeated.

But he was quite dumb. She fetched him a sharp slap on the face. He started, and his eyes widened. Then his face darkened with defiance, after all.

"Do you hear?" she repeated.

He only looked at her with hostile eyes.

"Speak!" she said, putting her face devilishly near his.

"What?" he said, almost overcome.

"You've got to *choose*!" she cried, as if it were some terrible menace, and as if it hurt her that she could not exact more.

"What?" he said, in fear.

"Choose your girl, Coddy. You've got to choose her now.

And you'll get your neck broken if you play any more of your tricks, my boy. You're settled now."

There was a pause. Again he averted his face. He was cunning in his overthrow. He did not give in to them really—no, not if they tore him to bits.

"All right, then," he said, "I choose Annie." His voice was strange and full of malice. Annie let go of him as if he had been a hot coal.

"He's chosen Annie!" said the girls in chorus.

"Me!" cried Annie. She was still kneeling, but away from him. He was still lying, prostrate, with averted face. The girls grouped uneasily around.

"Me!" repeated Annie, with a terrible bitter accent.

Then she got up, drawing away from him with strange disgust and bitterness.

"I wouldn't touch him," she said.

But her face quivered with a kind of agony, she seemed as if she would fall. The other girls turned aside. He remained lying on the floor, with his torn clothes and bleeding, averted face.

"Oh, if he's chosen——" said Polly.

"I don't want him—he can choose again," said Annie, with the same rather bitter hopelessness.

"Get up," said Polly, lifting his shoulder. "Get up."

He rose slowly, a strange, ragged, dazed creature. The girls eyed him from a distance, curiously, furtively, dangerously.

"Who wants him?" cried Laura, roughly.

"Nobody," they answered, with contempt. Yet each of them waited for him to look at her, hoped he would look at her. All except Annie, and something was broken in her.

He, however, kept his face closed and averted from them all. There was a silence of the end. He picked up the torn pieces of his tunic, without knowing what to do with them. The girls stood about uneasily, flushed, panting, tidying their hair and the dress unconsciously, and watching him. He looked at none of them. He espied his cap in a corner, and went and picked it up. He put it on his head, and one of the girls burst into a shrill, hysteric laugh at the sight he presented. He, however, took no heed, but went straight to where his overcoat hung on a peg. The girls moved away from contact with him as if he had been an electric wire. He put on his coat and buttoned it down. Then he rolled his tunic-rags into a bundle, and stood before the locked door, dumbly.

"Open the door, somebody," said Laura.

"Annie's got the key," said one.

Annie silently offered the key to the girls. Nora unlocked the door.

"Tit for tat, old man," she said. "Show yourself a man, and don't bear a grudge."

But without a word or sign he had opened the door and gone, his face closed, his head dropped.

"That'll learn him," said Laura.

"Coddy!" said Nora.

"Shut up, for God's sake!" cried Annie fiercely, as if in torture.

"Well, I'm about ready to go, Polly. Look sharp!" said Muriel.

The girls were all anxious to be off. They were tidying themselves hurriedly, with mute, stupefied faces.

Because of the war, women were for the first time doing jobs such as this on a large scale, demonstrating their equality and power. Lawrence sensed what this was meaning in many aspects of British society; and his sympathies in this story seem divided. We sympathize with the girls in wanting to take John Thomas down a peg or two; but we are meant to be rather horrified at the fury of their revenge.

Notice the dialogue throughout the story; without showing-off, it is skilfully realistic, making characters and situation convincing.

"Cinemas" in these early days of film were booths on the fairgrounds in which a few flickering pictures would be projected, as a novelty, not as an art. In describing the flirtation between Annie and John Thomas Lawrence's taste seems to me excellent: he is honest and good-humoured, and makes us recognize the warmth of the relationship, without being slick, or sentimental, or inappropriately poetic.

Why, when John Thomas comes into the waiting-room, is Annie silent for so long? Why, later, is she the leader of the attack? And why, at the end, is "something broken in her"?

Who wins the battle? What is the turning-point?

FOR FURTHER READING: Anyone can enjoy many of Lawrence's *Poems*, which are vivid and direct and avoid pretence of any kind; and also many stories, such as *Odour of Chrysanthemums, Fanny and Annie, Monkey Nuts, Samson and Delilah, The White Stocking* and others. And as a novelist Lawrence has been, I think, unequalled this century; but his best work is fully adult and written in a new, fairly difficult manner. One of the simplest and best is *Sons and Lovers*, which is at least partly autobiographical; and the later *The Lost Girl* is not difficult reading.

The collected works are published by Heinemann, and most are reprinted in Penguins.

ERNEST HEMINGWAY

Hemingway was born in Chicago in 1898 and died in 1961. People disagree considerably over the merit of his work, as perhaps readers will over this story, which is typical to the extent that it is very short and restrained and deals with violent realities, of birth and death and life, which we tend to shy away from. This is not a difficult story, but neither is it a comfortable one, and some readers may not have encountered anything like it before. Read it slowly, seeing that Hemingway has deliberately left much for *you* to imagine. He asks you also for a sympathy, and a respect, which I hope you will feel.

Indian Camp

At the lake shore there was another rowboat drawn up. The two Indians stood waiting.

Nick and his father got in the stern of the boat and the Indians shoved it off and one of them got in to row. Uncle George sat in the stern of the camp rowboat. The young Indian shoved the camp boat off and got in to row Uncle George.

The two boats started off in the dark. Nick heard the oarlocks of the other boat quite a way ahead of them in the mist. The Indians rowed with quick choppy strokes. Nick lay back with his father's arm around him. It was cold on the water. The Indian who was rowing them was working very hard, but the other boat moved farther ahead in the mist all the time.

"Where are we going, Dad?" Nick asked.

"Over to the Indian camp. There is an Indian lady very sick."

"Oh," said Nick.

Across the bay they found the other boat beached. Uncle George was smoking a cigar in the dark. The young Indian pulled the boat way up on the beach. Uncle George gave both the Indians cigars.

They walked up from the beach through a meadow that was soaking wet with dew, following the young Indian who carried a lantern. Then they went into the woods and followed a trail that led to the logging road that ran back into the hills. It was much lighter on the logging road as the timber was cut away on both sides. The young Indian stopped and blew out his lantern and they all walked on along the road.

They came around a bend and a dog came out barking. Ahead were the lights of the shanties where the Indian bark-peelers lived. More dogs rushed out at them. The two Indians sent them back to the shanties. In the shanty nearest the road there was a light in the window. An old woman stood in the doorway holding a lamp.

Inside on a wooden bunk lay a young Indian woman. She had been trying to have her baby for two days. All the old women in the camp had been helping her. The men had moved off up the road to sit in the dark and smoke out of range of the noise she made. She screamed just as Nick and the two Indians followed his father and Uncle George into the shanty.

She lay in the lower bunk, very big under a quilt. Her head was turned to one side. In the upper bunk was her husband. He had cut his foot very badly with an axe three days before. He was smoking a pipe. The room smelled very bad.

147

Nick's father ordered some water to be put on the stove, and while it was heating he spoke to Nick.

"This lady is going to have a baby, Nick," he said.

"I know," said Nick.

"You don't know," said his father. "Listen to me. What she is going through is called being in labour. The baby wants to be born and she wants it to be born. All her muscles are trying to get the baby born. That is what is happening when she screams."

"I see," Nick said.

Just then the woman cried out.

"Oh, Daddy, can't you give her something to make her stop screaming?" asked Nick.

"No. I haven't any anaesthetic," his father said. "But her screams are not important. I don't hear them because they are not important."

The husband in the upper bunk rolled over against the wall.

The woman in the kitchen motioned to the doctor that the water was hot. Nick's father went into the kitchen and poured about half of the water out of the big kettle into a basin. Into the water left in the kettle he put several things he unwrapped from a handkerchief.

"Those must boil," he said, and began to scrub his hands in the basin of hot water with a cake of soap he had brought from the camp. Nick watched his father's hands scrubbing each other with the soap. While his father washed his hands very carefully and thoroughly, he talked.

"You see, Nick, babies are supposed to be born head first, but sometimes they're not. When they're not they make a lot of trouble for everybody. Maybe I'll have to operate on this lady. We'll know in a little while."

When he was satisfied with his hands he went in and went to work.

148

"Pull back that quilt, will you, George?" he said. "I'd rather not touch it."

Later when he started to operate Uncle George and three Indian men held the woman still. She bit Uncle George on the arm and Uncle George said, "Damn squaw bitch!" and the young Indian who had rowed Uncle George over laughed at him. Nick held the basin for his father. It took a long time.

His father picked the baby up and slapped it to make it breathe and handed it to the old woman.

"See, it's a boy, Nick," he said. "How do you like being an interne?"

Nick said, "All right." He was looking away so as not to see what his father was doing.

"There. That gets it," said his father and put something into the basin.

Nick didn't look at it.

"Now," his father said, "there's some stitches to put in. You can watch this or not, Nick, just as you like. I'm going to sew up the incision I made."

Nick did not watch. His curiosity had been gone for a long time.

His father finished and stood up. Uncle George and the three Indian men stood up. Nick put the basin out in the kitchen.

Uncle George looked at his arm. The young Indian smiled reminiscently.

"I'll put some peroxide on that, George," the doctor said.

He bent over the Indian woman. She was quiet now and her eyes were closed. She looked very pale. She did not know what had become of the baby or anything.

"I'll be back in the morning," the doctor said, standing up. "The nurse should be here from St. Ignace by noon and she'll bring everything we need."

He was feeling exalted and talkative as football players are in the dressing-room after a game.

"That's one for the medical journal, George," he said. "Doing a Caesarian with a jack-knife and sewing it up with nine-foot, tapered gut leaders."

Uncle George was standing against the wall, looking at his arm.

"Oh, you're a great man, all right," he said.

"Ought to have a look at the proud father. They're usually the worst sufferers in these little affairs," the doctor said. "I must say he took it all pretty quietly."

He pulled back the blanket from the Indian's head. His hand came away wet. He mounted on the edge of the lower bunk with the lamp in one hand and looked in. The Indian lay with his face to the wall. His throat had been cut from ear to ear. The blood had flowed down into a pool where his body sagged the bunk. His head rested on his left arm. The open razor lay, edge up, in the blankets.

"Take Nick out of the shanty, George," the doctor said.

There was no need of that. Nick, standing in the door of the kitchen, had a good view of the upper bunk when his father, the lamp in one hand, tipped the Indian's head back.

It was just beginning to be daylight when they walked along the logging road back towards the lake.

"I'm terribly sorry I brought you along, Nickie," said his father, all his post-operative exhilaration gone. "It was an awful mess to put you through."

"Do ladies always have such a hard time having babies?" Nick asked.

"No, that was very, very exceptional."

"Why did he kill himself, Daddy?"

"I don't know, Nick. He couldn't stand things, I guess."

"Do many men kill themselves, Daddy?"

"Not very many, Nick."

"Do many women?"

"Hardly ever."

"Don't they ever?"

"Oh, yes. They do sometimes."

"Daddy?"

"Yes."

"Where did Uncle George go?"

"He'll turn up all right."

"Is dying hard, Daddy?"

"No, I think it's pretty easy, Nick. It all depends."

They were seated in the boat, Nick in the stern, his father rowing. The sun was coming up over the hills. A bass jumped, making a circle in the water. Nick trailed his hand in the water. It felt warm in the sharp chill of the morning.

In the early morning on the lake sitting in the stern of the boat with his father rowing, he felt quite sure that he would never die.

INTERNE: *(page 149) a medical student acting as an assistant to a doctor or surgeon. Do you think it was wrong of his father to take Nick along and accept his help? Was it an experience Nick would have been better without?*

Why should anyone want to write, or read, such a story? How, if at all, does it affect you?

Hemingway's writing is one of the extreme examples in literature of simplicity of style; he firmly refuses to use complicated sentence structures, elaborate language, or an analytical approach. What is gained by this; and what lost?

FOR FURTHER READING: *The First Forty-Nine Stories*, published by Jonathan Cape; many of these are reprinted in the Penguins *The Snows of Kilimanjaro* and *Men Without Women*.

All of Hemingway's work is in some way concerned with

courage; he himself, in war and peace, constantly showed his courage—or bravado—and at his best he writes of danger and pain with great compassion. The novel to start with is undoubtedly the short *The Old Man and the Sea*. (Jonathan Cape.)

F. SCOTT FITZGERALD

Scott Fitzgerald was born in America in 1896, and died in 1940. During his lifetime he had tremendous early success, and then became half forgotten, wasting his energies writing film-scripts too good to be produced. His personality had many of the characteristics of a glossy Hollywood musical: a warm gaiety, high ability—some of Fitzgerald's witty sentences are like brilliant tap-dancing—with a secret hollowness and desperation. At his best, however, he broke through the glossy surface of the "high society" he knew, to discover the sometimes tragic realities within; and he is now recognized as a major twentieth-century writer.

The Ice Palace was written when Fitzgerald was only twenty-three, about the time that he was married to Zelda Sayre, a beautiful girl, like Sally Carrol, from the Deep South. Being himself a Northerner the writer was perhaps amusing himself and Zelda here (a lot of stories get written this way), although humour is by no means the story's only quality.

The Ice Palace

I

The sunlight dripped over the house like golden paint over an art jar, and the freckling shadows here and there only intensified the rigour of the bath of light. The Butterworth and Larkin houses flanking were intrenched behind great stodgy trees; only the Happer house took the full sun, and all day long faced the dusty road-street with a tolerant kindly patience. This was the city of Tarleton in southernmost Georgia, September afternoon.

Up in her bedroom window Sally Carrol Happer rested her nineteen-year-old chin on a fifty-two-year-old sill and watched Clark Darrow's ancient Ford turn the corner. The car was hot—being partly metallic it retained all the heat it absorbed or evolved—and Clark Darrow sitting bolt upright at the wheel wore a pained, strained expression as though he considered himself a spare part, and rather likely to break. He laboriously crossed two dust ruts, the wheels squeaking indignantly at the encounter, and then with a terrifying expression he gave the steering-gear a final wrench and deposited self and car approximately in front of the Happer steps. There was a plaintive heaving sound, a death-rattle, followed by a short silence; and then the air was rent by a startling whistle.

Sally Carrol gazed down sleepily. She started to yawn, but finding this quite impossible unless she raised her chin from the window-sill, changed her mind and continued silently to regard the car, whose owner sat brilliantly if perfunctorily at attention as he waited for an answer to his signal. After a moment the whistle once more split the dusty air.

"Good mawnin'."

With difficulty Clark twisted his tall body round and bent a distorted glance on the window.

"'Tain't mawnin', Sally Carrol."

"Isn't it, sure enough?"

"What you doin'?"

"Eatin' 'n apple."

"Come on go swimmin'—want to?"

"Reckon so."

"How 'bout hurryin' up?"

"Sure enough."

Sally Carrol sighed voluminously and raised herself with profound inertia from the floor, where she had been occupied in alternately destroying parts of a green apple and painting paper dolls for her younger sister. She approached a mirror, regarded her expression with a pleased and pleasant languor, dabbed two spots of rouge on her lips and a grain of powder on her nose, and covered her bobbed corn-coloured hair with a rose-littered sunbonnet. Then she kicked over the painting-water, said, "Oh, damn!"—but let it lay—and left the room.

"How you, Clark?" she inquired a minute later as she slipped nimbly over the side of the car.

"Mighty fine, Sally Carrol."

"Where we go swimmin'?"

"Out to Walley's Pool. Told Marylyn we'd call by an' get her an' Joe Ewing."

Clark was dark and lean, and when on foot was rather inclined to stoop. His eyes were ominous and his expression somewhat petulant except when startlingly illuminated by one of his frequent smiles. Clark had "an income"—just enough to keep himself in ease and his car in gasoline—and he had spent the two years since he graduated from Georgia Tech in dozing round the lazy streets of his home town, discussing how he could best invest his capital for an immediate fortune.

Hanging round he found not at all difficult; a crowd of little girls had grown up beautifully, the amazing Sally Carrol foremost among them; and they enjoyed being swum with and danced with and made love to in the flower-filled summery evenings—and they all liked Clark immensely. When feminine company palled there were half a dozen youths who were always just about to do something, and meanwhile were quite willing to join him in a few holes of golf, or a game of billiards, or the consumption of a quart of "hard yella licker". Every once in a while one of these contemporaries made a farewell round of calls before going up to New York or Philadelphia or Pittsburgh to go into business, but mostly they just stayed round in this languid paradise of dreamy skies and firefly evenings and noisy niggery street fairs—and especially of gracious, soft-voiced girls, who were brought up on memories instead of money.

The Ford having been excited into a sort of restless resentful life Clark and Sally Carrol rolled and rattled down Valley Avenue into Jefferson Street, where the dust road became a pavement; along opiate Millicent Place, where there were half a dozen prosperous substantial mansions; and on into the down-town section. Driving was perilous here, for it was shopping time; the population idled casually across the streets and a drove of low-moaning oxen were being urged along in front of a placid street-car; even the shops seemed only yawning their doors and blinking their windows in the sunshine before retiring into a state of utter and finite coma.

"Sally Carrol," said Clark suddenly, "is it a fact you're engaged?"

She looked at him quickly.

"Where'd you hear that?"

"Sure enough, you engaged?"

"'At's a nice question!"

"Girl told me you were engaged to a Yankee you met up in Asheville last summer."

Sally Carrol sighed.

"Never saw such an old town for rumours."

"Don't marry a Yankee, Sally Carrol. We need you round here." Sally Carrol was silent a moment.

"Clark," she demanded suddenly, "who on earth shall I marry?"

"I offer my services."

"Honey, you couldn't support a wife," she answered cheerfully. "Anyway, I know you too well to fall in love with you."

"'At doesn't mean you ought to marry a Yankee," he persisted.

"S'pose I love him?"

He shook his head.

"You couldn't. He'd be a lot different from us, every way."

He broke off as he halted the car in front of a rambling, dilapidated house. Marylyn Wade and Joe Ewing appeared in the doorway.

"'Lo, Sally Carrol."

"Hi!"

"How you-all?"

"Sally Carrol," demanded Marylyn as they started off again, "you engaged?"

"Lawdy, where'd all this start? Can't I look at a man 'thout everybody in town engagin' me to him?"

Clark stared straight in front of him at a bolt on the clattering wind-shield.

"Sally Carrol," he said with a curious intensity, "don't you like us?"

"What?"

"Us down here?"

"Why, Clark, you know I do. I adore all you boys."

"Then why you gettin' engaged to a Yankee?"

"Clark, I don't know. I'm not sure what I'll do, but—well, I want to go places and see people. I want my mind to grow. I want to live where things happen on a big scale."

"What you mean?"

"Oh, Clark, I love you, and I love Joe here, and Ben Arrot, and you-all, but you'll—you'll——"

"We'll all be failures?"

"Yes. I don't mean only money failures, but just sort of—of ineffectual and sad, and—oh, how can I tell you?"

"You mean because we stay here in Tarleton?"

"Yes, Clark; and because you like it and never want to change things or think or go ahead."

He nodded and she reached over and pressed his hand.

"Clark," she said softly, "I wouldn't change you for the world. You're sweet the way you are. The things that'll make you fail I'll love always—the living in the past, the lazy days and nights you have, and all your carelessness and generosity."

"But you're goin' away?"

"Yes—because I couldn't ever marry you. You've a place in my heart no one else could ever have, but tied down here I'd get restless. I'd feel I was—wastin' myself. There's two sides to me, you see. There's the sleepy old side you love; an' there's a sort of energy—the feelin' that makes me do wild things. That's the part of me that may be useful somewhere, that'll last when I'm not beautiful any more."

She broke off with characteristic suddenness and sighed, "Oh, sweet cooky!" as her mood changed.

Half closing her eyes and tipping back her head till it rested on the seat-back she let the savory breeze fan her eyes and ripple the fluffy curls of her bobbed hair. They were in the country now, hurrying between tangled growths of bright-green coppice and grass and tall trees that sent sprays of foliage to hang a cool welcome over the road. Here and there they passed a battered Negro cabin, its oldest white-haired inhabitant smoking a corncob pipe beside the door, and half a dozen scantily clothed pickaninnies parading tattered dolls on the wild-grown grass in front. Farther out were lazy cotton-fields, where even the workers seemed intangible shadows lent by the sun to the earth, not for toil, but to while away some age-old tradition in the golden September fields. And round the drowsy picturesqueness, over the trees and shacks and muddy rivers, flowed the heat, never hostile, only comforting, like a great warm nourishing bosom for the infant earth.

"Sally Carrol, we're here!"

"Poor chile's soun' asleep."

"Honey, you dead at last outa sheer laziness?"

"Water, Sally Carrol! Cool water waitin' for you!"

Her eyes opened sleepily.

"Hi!" she murmured, smiling.

II

In November Harry Bellamy, tall, broad, and brisk, came down from his Northern city to spend four days. His intention was to settle a matter which had been hanging fire since he and Sally Carrol had met in Asheville, North Carolina, in mid-summer. The settlement took only a quiet afternoon and an evening in front of a glowing open fire, for Harry Bellamy had everything she wanted; and, besides, she loved him—loved him with that side of her she kept especially for loving. Sally Carrol had several rather clearly defined sides.

On his last afternoon they walked, and she found their steps tending half-consciously towards one of her favourite haunts, the cemetery. When it came in sight, grey-white and golden-green under the cheerful late sun, she paused, ir-resolute, by the iron gate.

"Are you mournful by nature, Harry?" she asked with a faint smile.

"Mournful? Not I."

"Then let's go in here. It depresses some folks, but I like it."

They passed through the gateway and followed a path that led through a wavy valley of graves—dusty-grey and mouldy for the fifties; quaintly•carved with flowers and jars for the seventies; ornate and hideous for the nineties, with fat marble cherubs lying in sodden sleep on stone pillows, and great impossible growths of nameless granite flowers. Occasionally they saw a kneeling figure with tributary flowers, but over most of the graves lay silence and withered leaves with only the fragrance that their own shadowy memories could awaken in living minds.

They reached the top of a hill where they were fronted by a tall, round head-stone, freckled with dark spots of damp and half grown over with vines.

"Margery Lee," she read; "1844–1873. Wasn't she nice? She died when she was twenty-nine. Dear Margery Lee," she added softly. "Can't you see her, Harry?"

"Yes, Sally Carrol."

He felt a little hand insert itself into his.

"She was dark, I think; and she always wore her hair with a ribbon in it, and gorgeous hoop-skirts of alice blue and old rose."

"Yes."

"Oh, she was sweet, Harry! And she was the sort of girl born to stand on a wide, pillared porch and welcome folks in. I think perhaps a lot of men went away to war meanin' to come back to her; but maybe none of 'em ever did."

He stooped down close to the stone, hunting for any record of marriage.

"There's nothing here to show."

"Of course not. How could there be anything there better than just 'Margery Lee', and that eloquent date?"

She drew close to him and an unexpected lump came into his throat as her yellow hair brushed his cheek.

"You see how she was, don't you, Harry?"

"I see," he agreed gently. "I see through your precious eyes. You're beautiful now, so I know she must have been."

Silent and close they stood, and he could feel her shoulders trembling a little. An ambling breeze swept up the hill and stirred the brim of her floppidy hat.

"Let's go down there!"

She was pointing to a flat stretch on the other side of the

hill where along the green turf were a thousand greyish-white crosses stretching in endless, ordered rows like the stacked arms of a battalion.

"Those are the Confederate dead," said Sally Carrol simply.

They walked along and read the inscriptions, always only a name and a date, sometimes quite indecipherable.

"The last row is the saddest—see, 'way over there. Every cross has just a date on it, and the word 'Unknown'."

She looked at him and her eyes brimmed with tears.

"I can't tell how real it is to me, darling—if you don't know."

"How you feel about it is beautiful to me."

"No, no, it's not me, it's them—that old time that I've tried to have live in me. These were just men, unimportant evidently or they wouldn't have been 'unknown'; but they died for the most beautiful thing in the world—the dead South. You see," she continued, her voice still husky, her eyes glistening with tears, "people have these dreams they fasten on to things, and I've always grown up with that disillusions comin' to me. I've tried in a way to live up to those past standards of noblesse oblige—there's just the last remnants of it, you know, like the roses of an old garden dying all round us—streaks of strange courtliness and chivalry in some of these boys an' stories I used to hear from a Confederate soldier who lived next door, and a few old darkies. Oh, Harry, there was something, there was something! I couldn't ever make you understand, but it was there."

"I understand," he assured her again quietly.

Sally Carrol smiled and dried her eyes on the tip of a handkerchief protruding from his breast pocket.

"You don't feel depressed, do you, lover? Even when I cry I'm happy here, and I get a sort of strength from it."

Hand in hand they turned and walked slowly away. Finding

soft grass she drew him down to a seat beside her with their backs against the remnants of a low broken wall.

"Wish those three old women would clear out," he complained. "I want to kiss you, Sally Carrol."

"Me, too."

They waited impatiently for the three bent figures to move off, and then she kissed him until the sky seemed to fade out and all her smiles and tears to vanish in an ecstasy of eternal seconds.

Afterwards they walked slowly back together, while on the corners twilight played at somnolent black-and-white checkers with the end of day.

"You'll be up about mid-January," he said, "and you've got to stay a month at least. It'll be slick. There's a winter carnival on, and if you've never really seen snow it'll be like fairy-land to you. There'll be skating and ski-ing and tobogganing and sleigh-riding, and all sorts of torchlight parades on snow-shoes. They haven't had one for years, so they're going to make it a knock-out."

"Will I be cold, Harry?" she asked suddenly.

"You certainly won't. You may freeze your nose, but you won't be shivery cold. It's hard and dry, you know."

"I guess I'm a summer child. I don't like any cold I've ever seen."

She broke off and they were both silent for a minute.

"Sally Carrol," he said very slowly, "what do you say to—March?"

"I say I love you."

"March?"

"March, Harry."

III

All night in the Pullman it was very cold. She rang for the porter to ask for another blanket, and when he couldn't give her one she tried vainly, by squeezing down into the bottom of her berth and doubling back the bedclothes, to snatch a few hours' sleep. She wanted to look her best in the morning.

She rose at six and sliding uncomfortably into her clothes stumbled up to the diner for a cup of coffee. The snow had filtered into the vestibules and covered the floor with a slippery coating. It was intriguing, this cold, it crept in everywhere. Her breath was quite visible and she blew into the air with a naïve enjoyment. Seated in the diner she stared out the window at white hills and valleys and scattered pines whose every branch was a green platter for a cold feast of snow. Sometimes a solitary farmhouse would fly by, ugly and bleak and lone on the white waste; and with each one she had an instant of chill compassion for the souls shut in there waiting for spring.

As she left the diner and swayed back into the Pullman she experienced a surging rush of energy and wondered if she was feeling the bracing air of which Harry had spoken. This was the North, the North—her land now!

> "*Then blow, ye winds, heigho!*
> *A-roving I will go*,"

she chanted exultantly to herself.

"What's 'at?" inquired the porter politely.

"I said: 'Brush me off'."

The long wires of the telegraph-poles doubled; two tracks ran up beside the train—three—four; came a succession of white-roofed houses, a glimpse of a trolley-car with frosted windows, streets—more streets—the city.

She stood for a dazed moment in the frosty station before she saw three fur-bundled figures descending upon her.

"There she is!"

"Oh, Sally Carrol!"

Sally Carrol dropped her bag.

"Hi!"

A faintly familiar icy-cold face kissed her, and then she was in a group of faces all apparently emitting great clouds of heavy smoke; she was shaking hands. There were Gordon, a short, eager man of thirty who looked like an amateur knocked-about model for Harry, and his wife, Myra, a listless lady with flaxen hair under a fur automobile cap. Almost immediately Sally Carrol thought of her as vaguely Scandinavian. A cheerful chauffeur adopted her bag, and amid ricochets of half-phrases, exclamations, and perfunctory listless "my dears" from Myra, they swept each other from the station.

Then they were in a sedan bound through a crooked succession of snowy streets where dozens of little boys were hitching sleds behind grocery wagons and automobiles.

"Oh," cried Sally Carrol, "I want to do that! Can we, Harry?"

"That's for kids. But we might——"

"It looks like such a circus!" she said regretfully.

Home was a rambling frame house set on a white lap of snow, and there she met a big, grey-haired man of whom she approved, and a lady who was like an egg, and who kissed her—these were Harry's parents. There was a breathless indescribable hour crammed full of half-sentences, hot water, bacon and eggs and confusion; and after that she was alone with Harry in the library, asking him if she dared smoke.

It was a large room with a Madonna over the fireplace and rows upon rows of books in covers of light gold and dark gold and shiny red. All the chairs had little lace squares where one's head should rest, the couch was just comfortable, the books looked as if they had been read—some—and Sally Carrol had an instantaneous vision of the battered old library at home, with her father's huge medical books, and the oil-paintings of her three great-uncles, and the old couch that had been mended up for forty-five years and was still luxurious to dream in. This room struck her as being neither attractive nor particularly otherwise. It was simply a room with a lot of fairly expensive things in it that all looked about fifteen years old.

"What do you think of it up here?" demanded Harry eagerly. "Does it surprise you? Is it what you expected, I mean?"

"You are, Harry," she said quietly, and reached out her arms to him.

But after a brief kiss he seemed anxious to extort enthusiasm from her.

"The town, I mean. Do you like it? Can you feel the pep in the air?"

"Oh, Harry," she laughed, "you'll have to give me time. You can't just fling questions at me."

She puffed at her cigarette with a sigh of contentment.

"One thing I want to ask you," he began rather apologetically; "you Southerners put quite an emphasis on family, and all that—not that it isn't quite all right, but you'll find it a little different here. I mean—you'll notice a lot of things that'll seem to you sort of vulgar display at first, Sally Carrol; but just remember that this is a three-generation town. Everybody has a father, and about half of us have grandfathers. Back of that we don't go."

"Of course," she murmured.

"Our grandfathers, you see, founded the place, and a lot of them had to take some pretty queer jobs while they were doing the founding. For instance, there's one woman who at present is about the social model for the town; well, her father was the first public ash man—things like that."

"Why," said Sally Carrol, puzzled, "did you s'pose I was goin' to make remarks about people?"

"Not at all," interrupted Harry; "and I'm not apologizing for anyone either. It's just that—well, a Southern girl came up here last summer and said some unfortunate things, and—oh, I just thought I'd tell you."

Sally Carrol felt suddenly indignant—as though she had been unjustly spanked—but Harry evidently considered the subject closed, for he went on with a great surge of enthusiasm.

"It's carnival time, you know. First in ten years. And there's an ice palace they're building now that's the first they've had since eighty-five. Built out of blocks of the clearest ice they could find—on a tremendous scale."

She rose and walking to the window pushed aside the heavy Turkish *portières* and looked out.

"Oh!" she cried suddenly. "There's two little boys makin' a snow man! Harry, do you reckon I can go out an' help 'em?"

"You dream! Come here and kiss me."

She left the window rather reluctantly.

"I don't guess this is a very kissable climate, is it? I mean, it makes you so you don't want to sit round, doesn't it?"

"We're not going to. I've got a vacation for the first week you're here, and there's a dinner–dance tonight."

"Oh, Harry," she confessed, subsiding in a heap, half in his lap, half in the pillows, "I sure do feel confused. I haven't got an idea whether I'll like it or not, an' I don't know what people expect, or anythin'. You'll have to tell me, honey."

"I'll tell you," he said softly, "if you'll just tell me you're glad to be here."

"Glad—just awful glad!" she whispered, insinuating herself into his arms in her own peculiar way. "Where you are is home for me, Harry."

And as she said this she had the feeling for almost the first time in her life that she was acting a part.

That night, amid the gleaming candles of a dinner-party, where the men seemed to do most of the talking while the girls sat in a haughty and expensive aloofness, even Harry's presence on her left failed to make her feel at home.

"They're a good-looking crowd, don't you think?" he demanded. "Just look round. There's Spud Hubbard, tackle at Princeton last year, and Junie Morton—he and the red-haired fellow next to him were both Yale hockey captains; Junie was in my class. Why, the best athletes in the world come from these States round here. This is a man's country, I tell you. Look at John J. Fishburn!"

"Who's he?" asked Sally Carrol innocently.

"Don't you know?"

"I've heard the name."

"Greatest wheat man in the north-west, and one of the greatest financiers in the country."

She turned suddenly to a voice on her right.

"I guess they forgot to introduce us. My name's Roger Patton."

"My name is Sally Carrol Happer," she said graciously.

"Yes, I know. Harry told me you were coming."

"You a relative?"

"No, I'm a professor."

"Oh," she laughed.

"At the university. You're from the South, aren't you?"

"Yes; Tarleton, Georgia."

She liked him immediately—a reddish-brown moustache under watery blue eyes that had something in them that these other eyes lacked, some quality of appreciation. They exchanged stray sentences through dinner, and she made up her mind to see him again.

After coffee she was introduced to numerous good-looking young men who danced with conscious precision and seemed to take it for granted that she wanted to talk about nothing except Harry.

"Heavens," she thought, "they talk as if my being engaged made me older than they are—as if I'd tell their mothers on them!"

In the South an engaged girl, even a young married woman, expected the same amount of half-affectionate badinage and flattery that would be accorded a débutante, but here all that seemed banned. One young man, after getting well started on the subject of Sally Carrol's eyes, and how they had allured him ever since she entered the room, went into a violent confusion when he found she was visiting the Bellamys—was Harry's fiancée. He seemed to feel as though he had made some *risqué* and inexcusable blunder, became immediately formal, and left her at the first opportunity.

She was rather glad when Roger Patton cut in on her and suggested that they sit out a while.

"Well," he inquired, blinking cheerily, "how's Carmen from the South?"

"Mighty fine. How's—how's Dangerous Dan McGrew? Sorry, but he's the only Northener I know much about."

He seemed to enjoy that.

"Of course," he confessed, "as a professor of literature I'm not supposed to have read Dangerous Dan McGrew."

"Are you a native?"

"No, I'm a Philadelphian. Imported from Harvard to teach French. But I've been here ten years."

"Nine years, three hundred an' sixty-four days longer than me."

"Like it here?"

"Uh-huh. Sure do!"

"Really?"

"Well, why not? Don't I look as if I were havin' a good time?"

"I saw you look out the window a minute ago—and shiver."

"Just my imagination," laughed Sally Carrol. "I'm used to havin' everythin' quiet outside, an' sometimes I look out an' see a flurry of snow, an' it's just as if somethin' dead was movin'."

He nodded appreciatively.

"Ever been North before?"

"Spent two Julys in Asheville, North Carolina."

"Nice-looking crowd, aren't they?" suggested Patton, indicating the swirling floor.

Sally Carrol started. This had been Harry's remark.

"Sure are! They're—canine."

"What?"

She flushed.

"I'm sorry; that sounded worse than I meant it. You see I always think of people as feline or canine, irrespective of sex."

"Which arc you?"

"I'm feline. So are you. So are most Southern men an' most of these girls here."

"What's Harry?"

"Harry's canine distinctly. All the men I've met tonight seem to be canine."

"What does 'canine' imply? A certain conscious masculinity as opposed to subtlety?"

"Reckon so. I never analysed it—only I just look at people an' say 'canine' or 'feline' right off. It's right absurd, I guess."

"Not at all. I'm interested. I used to have a theory about these people. I think they're freezing up."

"What?"

"I think they're growing like Swedes—Ibsenesque, you know. Very gradually getting gloomy and melancholy. It's these long winters. Ever read any Ibsen?"

She shook her head.

"Well, you find in his characters a certain brooding rigidity. They're righteous, narrow, and cheerless, without infinite possibilities for great sorrow or joy."

"Without smiles or tears?"

"Exactly. That's my theory. You see there are thousands of Swedes up here. They come, I imagine, because the climate is very much like their own, and there's been a gradual mingling. They're probably not half a dozen here tonight, but—we've had four Swedish governors. Am I boring you?"

"I'm mighty interested."

"Your future sister-in-law is half Swedish. Personally I like her, but my theory is that Swedes react rather badly on us as a whole. Scandinavians, you know, have the largest suicide rate in the world."

"Why do you live here if it's so depressing?"

"Oh, it doesn't get me. I'm pretty well cloistered, and I suppose books mean more than people to me anyway."

"But writers all speak about the South being tragic. You know—Spanish señoritas, black hair and daggers an' haunting music."

He shook his head.

"No, the Northern races are the tragic races—they don't indulge in the cheering luxury of tears."

Sally Carrol thought of her graveyard. She supposed that that was vaguely what she had meant when she said it didn't depress her.

"The Italians are about the gayest people in the world—but it's a dull subject," he broke off. "Anyway, I want to tell you you're marrying a pretty fine man."

Sally Carrol was moved by an impulse of confidence.

"I know. I'm the sort of person who wants to be taken care of after a certain point, and I feel sure I will be."

"Shall we dance? You know," he continued as they rose, "it's encouraging to find a girl who knows what she's marrying for. Nine-tenths of them think of it as a sort of walking into a moving-picture sunset."

She laughed, and liked him immensely.

Two hours later on the way home she nestled near Harry in the back seat.

"Oh, Harry," she whispered, "it's so co-old!"

"But it's warm in here, darling girl."

"But outside it's cold; and, oh, that howling wind!"

She buried her face deep in his fur coat and trembled involuntarily as his cold lips kissed the tip of her ear.

IV

The first week of her visit passed in a whirl. She had her promised toboggan-ride at the back of an automobile through a chill January twilight. Swathed in furs she put in a morning tobogganing on the country-club hill; even tried ski-ing, to sail through the air for a glorious moment and then land in a tangled laughing bundle on a' soft snowdrift. She liked all the winter sports, except an afternoon spent snow-shoeing over a glaring plain under pale yellow sunshine, but she soon realized that these things were for children—that she was being humoured and that the enjoyment round her was only a reflection of her own.

At first the Bellamy family puzzled her. The men were reliable and she liked them; to Mr. Bellamy especially, with his iron-grey hair and energetic dignity, she took an immediate fancy, once she found that he was born in Kentucky; this made him a link between the old life and the new. But towards the women she felt a definite hostility. Myra, her future sister-in-law, seemed the essence of spiritless conventionality. Her conversation was so utterly devoid of personality that Sally Carrol, who came from a country where a certain amount of charm could be taken for granted in the women, was inclined to despise her.

"If those women aren't beautiful," she thought, "they're nothing. They just fade out when you look at them. They're glorified domestics. Men are the centre of every mixed group."

Lastly there was Mrs. Bellamy, whom Sally Carrol detested. The first day's impression of an egg had been confirmed—an egg with a cracked, veiny voice and such an ungracious dumpiness of carriage that Sally Carrol felt that if she once fell she would surely scramble. In addition, Mrs. Bellamy seemed to typify the town in being innately hostile to strangers. She called Sally Carrol "Sally", and could not be persuaded that the double name was anything more than a tedious ridiculous nickname. To Sally Carrol this shortening of her name was like presenting her to the public half clothed. She loved "Sally Carrol"; she loathed "Sally". She knew also that Harry's mother disapproved of her bobbed hair; and she had never dared smoke downstairs after that first day when Mrs. Bellamy had come into the library sniffing violently.

Of all the men she met she preferred Roger Patton, who was a frequent visitor at the house. He never again alluded to the Ibsenesque tendency of the populace, but when he came in one day and found her curled upon the sofa bent over "Peer Gynt" he laughed and told her to forget what he'd said—that it was all rot.

And then one afternoon in her second week she and Harry hovered on the edge of a dangerously steep quarrel. She considered that he precipitated it entirely, though the Serbia in the case was an unknown man who had not had his trousers pressed.

They had been walking homeward between mounds of high-piled snow and under a sun which Sally Carrol scarcely recognized. They passed a little girl done up in grey wool until she resembled a small Teddy bear, and Sally Carrol could not resist a gasp of maternal appreciation.

"Look! Harry!"

"What?"

"That little girl—did you see her face?"

"Yes, why?"

"It was red as a little strawberry. Oh, she was cute!"

"Why, your own face is almost as red as that already!

Everybody's healthy here. We're out in the cold as soon as we're old enough to walk. Wonderful climate!"

She looked at him and had to agree. He was mighty healthy-looking; so was his brother. And she had noticed the new red in her own cheeks that very morning.

Suddenly their glances were caught and held, and they stared for a moment at the street-corner ahead of them. A man was standing there, his knees bent, his eyes gazing upward with a tense expression as though he were about to make a leap towards the chilly sky. And then they both exploded into a shout of laughter, for coming closer they discovered it had been a ludicrous momentary illusion produced by the extreme bagginess of the man's trousers.

"Reckon that's one on us," she laughed.

"He must be a Southerner, judging by those trousers," suggested Harry mischievously.

"Why, Harry!"

Her surprised look must have irritated him.

"Those damn Southerners!"

Sally Carrol's eyes flashed.

"Don't call 'em that!"

"I'm sorry, dear," said Harry, malignantly apologetic, "but you know what I think of them. They're sort of—sort of degenerates—not at all like the old Southerners. They've lived so long down there with all the coloured people that they've gotten lazy and shiftless."

"Hush your mouth, Harry!" she cried angrily. "They're not! They may be lazy—anybody would be in that climate—but they're my best friends, an' I don't want to hear 'em criticized in any such sweepin' way. Some of 'em are the finest men in the world."

"Oh, I know. They're all right when they come North to college, but of all the hangdog, ill-dressed, slovenly lot I ever saw, a bunch of small-town Southerners are the worst!"

Sally Carrol was clinching her gloved hands and biting her lip furiously.

"Why," continued Harry, "there was one in my class at New Haven, and we all thought that at last we'd found the true type of Southern aristocrat, but it turned out he wasn't an aristocrat at all—just the son of a Northern carpet-bagger, who owned about all the cotton round Mobile."

"A Southerner wouldn't talk the way you're talking now," she said evenly.

"They haven't the energy!"

"Or the somethin' else."

"I'm sorry, Sally Carrol, but I've heard you say yourself that you'd never marry——"

"That's quite different. I told you I wouldn't want to tie my life to any of the boys that are around Tarleton now, but I never made any sweepin' generalities."

They walked along in silence.

"I probably spread it on a bit thick, Sally Carrol. I'm sorry."

She nodded but made no answer. Five minutes later as they stood in the hallway she suddenly threw her arms round him.

"Oh, Harry," she cried, her eyes brimming with tears, "let's get married next week. I'm afraid of having fusses like that. I'm afraid, Harry. It wouldn't be that way if we were married."

But Harry, being in the wrong, was still irritated.

"That'd be idiotic. We decided on March."

The tears in Sally Carrol's eyes faded; her expression hardened slightly.

"Very well—I suppose I shouldn't have said that."

Harry melted.

"Dear little nut!" he cried. "Come and kiss me and let's forget."

That very night at the end of a vaudeville performance the orchestra played "Dixie" and Sally Carrol felt something stronger and more enduring than her tears and smiles of the day brim up inside her. She leaned forward gripping the arms of her chair until her face grew crimson.

"Sort of get you, dear?" whispered Harry.

But she did not hear him. To the spirited throb of the violins and the inspiring beat of the kettledrums her own old ghosts were marching by and on into the darkness, and as fifes whistled and sighed in the low encore they seemed so nearly out of sight that she could have waved good-bye.

> *Away, away,*
> > *Away down South in Dixie!*
> *Away, away,*
> > *Away down South in Dixie!*

V

It was a particularly cold night. A sudden thaw had nearly cleared the streets the day before, but now they were traversed again with a powdery wraith of loose snow that travelled in wavy lines before the feet of the wind, and filled the lower air with a fine-particled mist. There was no sky—only a dark, ominous tent that draped in the tops of the streets and was in reality a vast approaching army of snowflakes—while over it all, chilling away the comfort from the brown-and-green glow of lighted windows and muffling the steady trot of the horse pulling their sleigh, interminably washed the north wind. It was a dismal town after all, she thought—dismal.

Sometimes at night it had seemed to her as though no one lived here—they had all gone long ago—leaving lighted houses to be covered in time by tombing heaps of sleet. Oh, if there should be snow on her grave! To be beneath great piles of it all winter long, where even her headstone would be a light shadow against light shadows. Her grave—a grave that should be flower-strewn and washed with sun and rain.

She thought again of those isolated country houses that her train had passed, and of the life there the long winter through —the ceaseless glare through the windows, the crust forming on the soft drifts of snow, finally the slow, cheerless melting, and the harsh spring of which Roger Patton had told her. Her spring—to lose it forever—with its lilacs and the lazy sweetness it stirred in her heart. She was laying away that spring— afterwards she would lay away that sweetness.

With a gradual insistence the storm broke. Sally Carrol felt a film of flakes melt quickly on her eyelashes, and Harry reached over a furry arm and drew down her complicated flannel cap. Then the small flakes came in skirmish-line, and the horse bent his neck patiently as a transparency of white appeared momentarily on his coat.

"Oh, he's cold, Harry," she said quickly.

"Who? The horse? Oh, no, he isn't. He likes it!"

After another ten minutes they turned a corner and came in sight of their destination. On a tall hill outlined in vivid glaring green against the wintry sky stood the ice palace. It was three stories in the air, with battlements and embrasures and narrow icicled windows, and the innumerable electric lights inside made a gorgeous transparency of the great central hall. Sally Carrol clutched Harry's hand under the fur robe.

"It's beautiful!" he cried excitedly. "My golly, it's beautiful, isn't it? They haven't had one here since eighty-five!"

Somehow the notion of there not having been one since eighty-five oppressed her. Ice was a ghost, and this mansion of it was surely peopled by those shades of the eighties, with pale faces and blurred snow-filled hair.

"Come on, dear," said Harry.

She followed him out of the sleigh and waited while he hitched the horse. A party of four—Gordon, Myra, Roger Patton, and another girl—drew up beside them with a mighty jingle of bells. There were quite a crowd already, bundled in fur or sheepskin, shouting and calling to each other as they moved through the snow, which was now so thick that people could scarcely be distinguished a few yards away.

"It's a hundred and seventy feet tall," Harry was saying to a muffled figure beside him as they trudged towards the entrance; "covers six thousand square yards."

She caught snatches of conversation: "One main hall"— "walls twenty to forty inches thick"—"and the ice cave has almost a mile of——"—"this Canuck who built it——"

They found their way inside, and dazed by the magic of the great crystal walls Sally Carrol found herself repeating over and over two lines from *Kubla Khan*:

> "*It was a miracle of rare device,*
> *A sunny pleasure-dome with caves of ice!*"

In the great glittering cavern with the dark shut out she took a seat on a wooden bench, and the evening's oppression lifted. Harry was right—it was beautiful; and her gaze travelled the smooth surface of the walls, the blocks for which had been selected for their purity and clearness to obtain this opalescent, translucent effect.

"Look! Here we go—oh, boy!" cried Harry.

A band in a far corner struck up "Hail, Hail, the Gang's All Here!" which echoed over to them in wild muddled acoustics, and then the lights suddenly went out; silence seemed to flow down the icy sides and sweep over them. Sally Carrol could still see her white breath in the darkness, and a dim row of pale faces over on the other side.

The music eased to a sighing complaint, and from outside drifted in the full-throated resonant chant of the marching clubs. It grew louder like some paean of a viking tribe traversing an ancient wild; it swelled—they were coming nearer; then a row of torches appeared, and another and another, and keeping time with their moccasined feet a long column of

177

grey-mackinawed figures swept in, snowshoes slung at their shoulders, torches soaring and flickering as their voices rose along the great walls.

The grey column ended and another followed, the light streaming luridly this time over red toboggan caps and flaming crimson mackinaws, and as they entered they took up the refrain; then came a long platoon of blue and white, of green, of white, of brown and yellow.

"Those white ones are the Wacouta Club," whispered Harry eagerly. "Those are the men you've met round at dances."

The volume of the voices grew; the great cavern was a phantasmagoria of torches waving in great banks of fire, of colours and the rhythm of soft-leather steps. The leading column turned and halted, platoon deployed in front of platoon until the whole procession made a solid flag of flame, and then from thousands of voices burst a mighty shout that filled the air like a crash of thunder, and sent the torches wavering. It was magnificent, it was tremendous! To Sally Carrol it was the North offering sacrifice on some mighty altar to the grey pagan God of Snow. As the shout died the band struck up again and there came more singing, and then long reverberating cheers by each club. She sat very quiet listening while the staccato cries rent the stillness; and then she started, for there was a volley of explosion, and great clouds of smoke went up here and there through the cavern—the flashlight photographers at work—and the council was over. With the band at their head the clubs formed in column once more, took up their chant, and began to march out.

"Come on!" shouted Harry. "We want to see the labyrinths downstairs before they turn the lights off!"

They all rose and started towards the chute—Harry and Sally Carrol in the lead, her little mitten buried in his big fur gauntlet! At the bottom of the chute was a long empty room of ice, with the ceiling so low they had to stoop—and their hands were parted. Before she realized what he intended Harry had darted down one of the half-dozen glittering passages that opened into the room and was only a vague receding blot against the green shimmer.

"Harry!" she called.

"Come on!" he cried back.

She looked round the empty chamber; the rest of the party had evidently decided to go home, were already outside somewhere in the blundering snow. She hesitated and then darted in after Harry.

"Harry!" she shouted.

She had reached a turning-point thirty feet down; she heard a faint muffled answer far to the left, and with a touch of panic fled towards it. She passed another turning, two more yawning alleys.

"Harry!"

No answer. She started to run straight forward, and then turned like lightning and sped back the way she had come, enveloped in a sudden icy terror.

She reached a turn—was it here?—took the left and came to what should have been the outlet into the long, low room, but it was only another glittering passage with darkness at the end. She called again but the walls gave back a flat, lifeless echo with no reverberations. Retracing her steps she turned another corner, this time following a wide passage. It was like the green lane between the parted waters of the Red Sea, like a damp vault connecting empty tombs.

She slipped a little now as she walked, for ice had formed on the bottom of her overshoes; she had to run her gloves along the half-slippery, half-sticky walls to keep her balance.

"Harry!"

Still no answer. The sound she made bounced mockingly down to the end of the passage.

Then on an instant the lights went out, and she was in complete darkness. She gave a small, frightened cry, and sank down into a cold little heap on the ice. She felt her left knee do something as she fell, but she scarcely noticed it as some deep terror far greater than any fear of being lost settled upon her. She was alone with this presence that came out of the North, the dreary loneliness that rose from ice-bound whalers in the Arctic seas, from smokeless, trackless wastes where were strewn the whitened bones of adventure. It was an icy breath of death; it was rolling down low across the land to clutch at her.

With a furious, despairing energy she rose again and started blindly down the darkness. She must get out. She might be lost in here for days, freeze to death and lie embedded in the ice like corpses she had read of, kept perfectly preserved until the melting of a glacier. Harry probably thought she had left with the others—he had gone by now; no one would know until late next day. She reached pitifully for the wall. Forty inches thick, they had said—forty inches thick!

"Oh!"

On both sides of her along the walls she felt things creeping, damp souls that haunted this palace, this town, this North.

"Oh, send somebody—send somebody!" she cried aloud.

Clark Darrow—he would understand; or Joe Ewing; she couldn't be left here to wander forever—to be frozen, heart, body, and soul. This her—this Sally Carrol! Why, she was a happy thing. She was a happy little girl. She liked warmth and summer and Dixie. These things were foreign—foreign.

"You're not crying," something said aloud. "You'll never cry any more. Your tears would just freeze; all tears freeze up here!"

She sprawled full length on the ice.

"Oh, God!" she faltered.

180

A long single file of minutes went by, and with a great weariness she felt her eyes closing. Then someone seemed to sit down near her and take her face in warm, soft hands. She looked up gratefully.

- "Why, it's Margery Lee," she crooned softly to herself. "I knew you'd come." It really was Margery Lee, and she was just as Sally Carrol had known she'd be, with a young, white brow, and wide, welcoming eyes, and a hoop-skirt of some soft material that was quite comforting to rest on.

"Margery Lee."

It was getting darker now and darker—all those tombstones ought to be repainted, sure enough, only that would spoil 'em, of course. Still, you ought to be able to see 'em.

Then after a succession of moments that went fast and then slow, but seemed to be ultimately resolving themselves into a multitude of blurred rays converging towards a pale-yellow sun, she heard a great cracking noise break her new-found stillness.

It was the sun, it was a light; a torch, and a torch beyond that, and another one, and voices; a face took flesh below the torch, heavy arms raised her, and she felt something on her cheek—it felt wet. Someone had seized her and was rubbing her face with snow. How ridiculous—with snow!

"Sally Carrol! Sally Carrol!"

It was Dangerous Dan McGrew; and two other faces she didn't know.

"Child, child! We've been looking for you two hours! Harry's half-crazy!"

Things came rushing back into place—the singing, the torches, the great shout of the marching clubs. She squirmed in Patton's arms and gave a long low cry.

"Oh, I want to get out of here! I'm going back home. Take me home"—her voice rose to a scream that sent a chill to Harry's heart as he came racing down the next passage—

"tomorrow!" she cried with delirious, unrestrained passion— "Tomorrow! Tomorrow! Tomorrow!"

VI

The wealth of golden sunlight poured a quite enervating yet oddly comforting heat over the house where day long it faced the dusty stretch of road. Two birds were making a great to-do in a cool spot found among the branches of a tree next door, and down the street a coloured woman was announcing herself melodiously as a purveyor of strawberries. It was April afternoon.

Sally Carrol Happer, resting her chin on her arm, and her arm on an old window-seat, gazed sleepily down over the spangled dust whence the heat waves were rising for the first time this spring. She was watching a very ancient Ford turn a perilous corner and rattle and groan to a jolting stop at the end of the walk. She made no sound, and in a minute a strident familiar whistle rent the air. Sally Carrol smiled and blinked.

"Good mawnin'."

A head appeared tortuously from under the car-top below.

"'Tain't mawnin', Sally Carrol."

"Sure enough!" she said in affected surprise. "I guess maybe not."

"What you doin'?"

"Eatin' green peach. 'Spect to die any minute."

Clark twisted himself a last impossible notch to get a view of her face.

"Water's warm as a kettla steam, Sally Carrol. Wanta go swimmin'?"

"Hate to move," sighed Sally Carrol lazily, "but I reckon so."

★

THE ICE PALACE

Even in England regional differences are strong, and some people find a change very difficult, particularly from south to north; but in America the difficulty is far more fundamental. Although probably the American Civil War (1861–5) was necessary and the Northern victory desirable, they left in the South resentments which still survive today. It isn't surprising that Sally Carrol should remember what was attractive in the Southern tradition; we all do this with our homeland; and the North to which Harry takes her is not the civilized East coast, with its own rich cultural traditions, but the huge and bleak Mid-West, of wide plains and hurriedly built industrial cities. This was Fitzgerald's birthplace; it is a measure of his skill that he makes us so sympathetic towards the Southern girl.

This is the kind of story which makes considerable use of symbolism. The ice palace itself represents what, in its cold and brilliance? Sally Carrol's near-burial in it is a grim warning of what? (Notice how the idea of peaceful burial is neatly continued throughout the story, from the slightly sentimental scene with Harry in the Tarleton cemetery.) Sally Carrol's eyes readily fill with tears, and she is childishly gay over tobogganing; Northern people, it is suggested, cannot smile or weep, and this is the most horrifying notion of all, when she is trapped in the ice palace—that emotions themselves should be killed. Similarly, who is it that rescues Sally Carrol (in more ways than one)? And why should it be this particular person? The fact that the author has obviously devised these supporting details is all part of the enjoyment.

FOR FURTHER READING: All Scott Fitzgerald's major work, originally published by the Bodley Head, is in Penguins; it is grown-up writing, but always lively and never really difficult: *The Diamond as Big as the Ritz* (stories), *The Great Gatsby*, *Tender is the Night*, and *The Last Tycoon*.

WILLIAM FAULKNER

Faulkner (1897–1962) lived most of his life in Mississippi, one of the most backward of the United States, and one in which the proportion of negroes is high. Through the eyes of Sally Carrol in *The Ice Palace* we saw a romantic, sentimental view of the Deep South; in Faulkner it is the sinister and horrific which are emphasized. His prose tends to resemble the local vegetation: steamy and over-grown; like Dylan Thomas, Faulkner delights in words, and loves the "impressive" cadence. This story, however, is straightforward; and it expresses strikingly the white Southerner's feelings when confronted by negro traditions.

Go Down, Moses

I

The face was black, smooth, impenetrable; the eyes had seen too much. The negroid hair had been treated so that it covered the skull like a cap, in a single neat-ridged sweep, with the appearance of having been lacquered, the part trimmed out with a razor, so that the head resembled a bronze head, imperishable and enduring. He wore one of those sports costumes called ensembles in the men's shop advertisements, shirt and trousers matching and cut from the same fawn-coloured material, and they had cost too much and were draped too much, with too many pleats; and he half lay on the steel cot in the steel cubicle just outside which an armed guard had stood for twenty hours now, smoking cigarettes and answering in a voice which was anything under the sun but a southern voice or even a negro voice, the questions of the spectacled young white man sitting with a broad census-taker's portfolio on the steel stool opposite:

"Samuel Worsham Beauchamp. Twenty-six. Born in the country near Jefferson, Mississippi. No family. No——"

"Wait." The census-taker wrote rapidly. "That's not the name you were sen—lived under in Chicago."

The other snapped the ash from his cigarette. "No. It was another guy killed the cop."

"All right. Occupation."

"Getting rich too fast."

"—none." The census-taker wrote rapidly. "Parents."

"Sure. Two. I don't remember them. My grandmother raised me."

"What's her name? Is she still living?"

"I don't know. Mollie Worsham Beauchamp. If she is, she's on Carothers Edmond's farm seventeen miles from Jefferson, Mississippi. That all?"

The census-taker closed the portfolio and stood up. He was a year or two younger than the other. "If they don't know who you are here, how will they know—how do you expect to get home?"

The other snapped the ash from his cigarette, lying on the steel cot in the fine Hollywood clothes and a pair of shoes better than the census-taker would ever own. "What will that matter to me?" he said.

So the census-taker departed; the guard locked the steel door again. And the other lay on the steel cot smoking until after a while they came and slit the expensive trousers and shaved the expensive coiffure and led him out of the cell.

II

On that same hot, bright July morning the same hot bright wind which shook the mulberry leaves just outside Gavin Stevens's window blew into the office too, contriving a semblance of coolness from what was merely motion. It fluttered among the county-attorney business on the desk and blew in the wild shock of prematurely white hair of the man who sat behind it—a thin, intelligent, unstable face, a rumpled linen suit from whose lapel a Phi Beta Kappa key dangled on a watch-chain—Gavin Stevens, Phi Beta Kappa, Harvard, Ph.D., Heidelberg, whose office was his hobby, although it made his living for him, and whose serious vocation was a twenty-two-year-old unfinished translation of the Old Testament back into classic Greek. Only his caller seemed impervious to it, though by appearance she should have owned in that breeze no more of weight and solidity than the intact ash of a scrap of burned paper—a little old negro woman with a shrunken, incredibly old face beneath a white headcloth and a black straw hat which would have fitted a child.

"Beauchamp?" Stevens said. "You live on Mr. Carothers Edmond's place."

"I done left," she said. "I come to find my boy." Then, sitting on the hard chair opposite him and without moving, she began to chant. "Roth Edmonds sold my Benjamin. Sold him in Egypt. Pharaoh got him——"

"Wait," Stevens said. "Wait, Aunty." Because memory, recollection, was about to mesh and click. "If you don't know where your grandson is, how do you know he's in trouble? Do you mean that Mr. Edmonds has refused to help you find him?"

"It was Roth Edmonds sold him," she said. "Sold him in

Egypt. I don't know whar he is. I just knows Pharaoh got him. And you the Law. I wants to find my boy."

"All right," Stevens said. "I'll try to find him. If you're not going back home, where will you stay in town? It may take some time, if you don't know where he went and you haven't heard from him in five years."

"I be staying with Hamp Worsham. He my brother."

"All right," Stevens said. He was not surprised. He had known Hamp Worsham all his life, though he had never seen the old negress before. But even if he had, he still would not have been surprised. They were like that. You could know two of them for years; they might even have worked for you for years, bearing different names. Then suddenly you learn by pure chance that they are brothers or sisters.

He sat in the hot motion which was not breeze and listened to her toiling slowly down the steep outside stairs, remembering the grandson. The papers of that business had passed across his desk before going to the District Attorney five or six years ago—Butch Beauchamp, as the youth had been known during the single year he had spent in and out of the city jail: the old negress's daughter's child, orphaned of his mother at birth and deserted by his father, whom the grandmother had taken and raised, or tried to. Because at nineteen he had quit the country and come to town and spent a year in and out of jail for gambling and fighting, to come at last under serious indictment for breaking and entering a store.

Caught red-handed, whereupon he had struck with a piece of iron pipe at the officer who surprised him and then lay on the ground where the officer had felled him with a pistol-butt, cursing through his broken mouth, his teeth fixed into something like furious laughter through the blood. Then two nights later he broke out of jail and was seen no more—a youth not yet twenty-one, with something in him from the father who begot and deserted him and who was now in the State

Penitentiary for manslaughter—some seed not only violent but dangerous and bad.

And that's who I am to find, save, Stevens thought. Because he did not for one moment doubt the old negress's instinct. If she had also been able to divine where the boy was and what his trouble was, he would not have been surprised, and it was only later that he thought to be surprised at how quickly he did find where the boy was and what was wrong.

His first thought was to telephone Carothers Edmonds, on whose farm the old negress's husband had been a tenant for years. But then, according to her, Edmonds had already refused to have anything to do with it. Then he sat perfectly still while the hot wind blew in his wild white mane. Now he comprehended what the old negress had meant. He remembered now that it was Edmonds who had actually sent the boy to Jefferson in the first place: he had caught the boy breaking into his commissary store and had ordered him off the place and had forbidden him ever to return. *And not the sheriff, the police*, he thought. *Something broader, quicker in scope. . . .* He rose and took his old fine worn panama and descended the outside stairs and crossed the empty square in the hot suspension of noon's beginning, to the office of the county newspaper. The editor was in—an older man but with hair less white than Stevens's, in a black string tie and an old-fashioned shirt and tremendously fat.

"An old nigger woman named Mollie Beauchamp," Stevens said. "She and her husband live on the Edmonds place. It's her grandson. You remember him—Butch Beauchamp, about five or six years ago, who spent a year in town, mostly in jail, until they finally caught him breaking into Rouncewell's store one night? Well, he's in worse trouble than that now, I don't doubt her at all. I just hope, for her sake as well as that of the great public whom I represent, that his present trouble is very bad and maybe final too——"

"Wait," the editor said. He didn't even need to leave his desk. He took the press association flimsy from its spike and handed it to Stevens. It was datelined from Joliet, Illinois, this morning:

> *Mississippi negro, on eve of execution for murder of Chicago policeman, exposes alias by completing census questionnaire. Samuel Worsham Beauchamp—*

Five minutes later Stevens was crossing again the empty square in which noon's hot suspension was that much nearer. He had thought that he was going home to his boarding-house for the noon meal, but he found that he was not. *"Besides, I didn't lock my office door,"* he thought. Only, how under the sun she could have got to town from those seventeen miles. She may even have walked. "So it seems I didn't mean what I said I hoped," he said aloud, mounting the outside stairs again, out of the hazy and now windless sunglare, and entered his office. He stopped. Then he said,

"Good morning, Miss Worsham."

She was quite old too—thin, erect, with a neat, old-time piling of white hair beneath a faded hat of thirty years ago, in rusty black, with a frayed umbrella faded now until it was green instead of black. She lived alone in the decaying house her father had left her, where she gave lessons in china-painting and, with the help of Hamp Worsham, descendant of one of her father's slaves, and his wife, raised chickens and vegetables for market.

"I came about Mollie," she said. "Mollie Beauchamp. She said that you——"

He told her while she watched him, erect on the hard chair where the old negress had sat, the rusty umbrella leaning against her knee. On her lap, beneath her folded hands, lay an old-fashioned beaded reticule almost as big as a suitcase. "He is to be executed tonight."

"Can nothing be done? Mollie and Hamp's parents belonged to my grandfather. Mollie and I were born in the same month. We grew up together as sisters would."

"I telephoned," Stevens said. "I talked to the Warden at Joliet, and to the District Attorney in Chicago. He had a fair trial, a good lawyer—of that sort. He had money. He was in a business called numbers, that people like him make money in." She watched him, erect and motionless. "He is a murderer, Miss Worsham. He shot that policeman in the back. A bad son of a bad father. He admitted, confessed it afterward."

"I know," she said. Then he realized that she was not looking at him, not seeing him at least. "It's terrible."

"So is murder terrible," Stevens said. "It's better this way." Then she was looking at him again.

"I wasn't thinking of him. I was thinking of Mollie. She mustn't know."

"Yes," Stevens said. "I have already talked with Mr. Wilmoth at the paper. He had agreed not to print anything. I will telephone the Memphis paper, but it's probably too late for that. . . . If we could just persuade her to go on back home this afternoon, before the Memphis paper. . . . Out there, where the only white person she ever sees is Mr. Edmonds, and I will telephone him; and even if the other darkies should hear about it, I'm sure they wouldn't. And then maybe in about two or three months I could go out there and tell her he is dead and buried somewhere in the North. . . ." This time she was watching him with such an expression that he ceased talking; she sat there, erect on the hard chair, watching him until he had ceased.

"She will want to take him back home with her," she said.

"Him?" Stevens said. "The body?" She watched him. The expression was neither shocked nor disapproving. It merely embodied some old, timeless affinity for blood and grief. Stevens thought: *She has walked to town in this heat. Unless*

190

Hamp brought her in the buggy he peddles eggs and vegetables from.

"He is the only child of her oldest daughter, her own dead first child. He must come home."

"He must come home," Stevens said as quietly. "I'll attend to it at once. I'll telephone at once."

"You are kind." For the first time she stirred, moved. He watched her hands draw the reticule towards her, clasping it. "I will defray the expenses. Can you give me some idea——?"

He looked her straight in the face. He told the lie without batting an eye, quickly and easily. "Ten or twelve dollars will cover it. They will furnish a box and there will be only the transportation."

"A box?" Again she was looking at him with that expression curious and detached, as though he were a child. "He is her grandson, Mr. Stevens. When she took him to raise, she gave him my father's name—Samuel Worsham. Not just a box, Mr. Stevens. I understand that can be done by paying so much a month."

"Not just a box," Stevens said. He said it in exactly the same tone in which he had said He must come home. "Mr. Edmonds will want to help. And I understand that old Luke Beauchamp had some money in the bank. And if you will permit me——"

"That will not be necessary," she said. He watched her open the reticule; he watched her count on to the desk twenty-five dollars in frayed bills and coins ranging down to nickels and dimes and pennies. "That will take care of the immediate expense. I will tell her—You are sure there is no hope?"

"I am sure. He will die tonight."

"I will tell her this afternoon that he is dead then."

"Would you like for me to tell her?"

"I will tell her," she said.

"Would you like for me to come out and see her, then, talk to her?"

"It would be kind of you." Then she was gone, erect, her feet crisp and light, almost brisk, on the stairs, ceasing. He telephoned again, to the Illinois warden, then to an undertaker in Joliet. Then once more he crossed the hot, empty square. He had only to wait a short while for the editor to return from dinner.

"We're bringing him home," he said. "Miss Worsham and you and me and some others. It will cost——"

"Wait," the editor said. "What others?"

"I don't know yet. It will cost about two hundred. I'm not counting the telephones; I'll take care of them myself. I'll get something out of Carothers Edmonds the first time I catch him; I don't know how much, but something. And maybe fifty around the square. But the rest of it is you and me, because she insisted on leaving twenty-five with me, which is just twice what I tried to persuade her it would cost and just exactly four times what she can afford to pay——"

"Wait," the editor said. "Wait."

"And he will come in on Number Four the day after tomorrow and we will meet it, Miss Worsham and his grandmother, the old nigger, in my car and you and me in yours. Miss Worsham and the old woman will take him back home, back where he was born. Or where the old woman raised him. Or where she tried to. And the hearse out there will be fifteen more, not counting the flowers——"

"Flowers?" the editor cried.

"Flowers," Stevens said. "Call the whole thing two hundred and twenty-five. And it will probably be mostly you and me. All right?"

"No it aint all right," the editor said. "But it don't look like I can help myself. By Jupiter," he said, "even if I could help myself, the novelty will be almost worth it. It will be the first time in my life I ever paid money for copy I had already promised beforehand I won't print."

"Have already promised beforehand you will not print," Stevens said. And during the remainder of that hot and now windless afternoon, while officials from the city hall, and justices of the peace and bailiffs come fifteen and twenty miles from the ends of the county, mounted the stairs to the empty office and called his name and cooled their heels a while and then went away and returned and sat again, fuming, Stevens passed from store to store and office to office about the square —merchant and clerk, proprietor and employee, doctor, dentist, lawyer, and barber—with his set and rapid speech: "It's to bring a dead nigger home. It's for Miss Worsham. Never mind about a paper to sign: just give me a dollar. Or half a dollar then. Or a quarter then."

And that night after supper he walked through the breathless and star-filled darkness to Miss Worsham's house on the edge of town and knocked on the paintless front door. Hamp Worsham admitted him—an old man, belly-bloated from the vegetables on which he and his wife and Miss Worsham all three mostly lived, with blurred old eyes and a fringe of white hair about the head and face of a Roman general.

"She expecting you," he said. "She say to kindly step up to the chamber."

"Is that where Aunt Mollie is?" Stevens asked.

"We all dar," Worsham said.

So Stevens crossed the lamplit hall (he knew that the entire house was still lighted with oil-lamps and there was no running water in it) and preceded the negro up the clean, paintless stairs beside the faded wallpaper, and followed the old negro along the hall and into the clean, spare bedroom with its unmistakable faint odour of old maidens. They were all there, as Worsham had said—his wife, a tremendous light-coloured woman again on a hard straight chair, the old negress sitting in the only rocking-chair beside the hearth on which even tonight a few ashes smouldered faintly.

She held a reed-stemmed clay pipe but she was not smoking it, the ash dead and white in the stained bowl, and actually looking at her for the first time, Stevens thought: *Good Lord, she's not as big as a ten-year-old child*. Then he sat too, so that the four of them—himself, Miss Worsham, the old negress and her brother—made a circle about the brick hearth on which the ancient symbol of human coherence and solidarity smouldered.

"He'll be home the day after tomorrow, Aunt Mollie," he said. The old negress didn't even look at him; she never had looked at him.

"He dead," she said. "Pharaoh got him."

"Oh yes, Lord," Worsham said. "Pharaoh got him."

"Done sold my Benjamin," the old negress said. "Sold him in Egypt." She began to sway faintly back and forth in the chair.

"Oh yes, Lord," Worsham said.

"Hush," Miss Worsham said. "Hush, Hamp."

"I telephoned Mr. Edmonds," Stevens said. "He will have everything ready when you get there."

"Roth Edmonds sold him," the old negress said. She swayed back and forth in the chair. "Sold my Benjamin."

"Hush," Miss Worsham said. "Hush, Mollie. Hush now."

"No," Stevens said. "No he didn't, Aunt Mollie. It wasn't Mr. Edmonds. Mr. Edmonds didn't——" *But she can't hear me*, he thought. She was not even looking at him. She had never looked at him.

"Sold my Benjamin," she said. "Sold him in Egypt."

"Sold him in Egypt," Worsham said.

"Roth Edmonds sold my Benjamin."

"Sold him to Pharaoh."

"Sold him to Pharaoh and now he dead."

"I'd better go," Stevens said. He rose quickly. Miss Worsham rose too, but he did not wait for her to precede him. He went down the hall fast, almost running; he did not even know whether she was following him or not. *Soon I will be outside,* he thought. *Then there will be air, space, breath.* Then he could hear her behind him—the crisp, light, brisk yet unhurried feet as he had heard them descending the stairs from his office, and beyond them the voices:

"Sold my Benjamin. Sold him in Egypt."

"Sold him in Egypt. Oh yes, Lord."

He descended the stairs, almost running. It was not far now; now he could smell and feel it: the breathing and simple dark, and now he could manner himself to pause and wait, turning at the door, watching Miss Worsham as she followed him to the door—the high, white, erect old-time head approaching through the old-time lamplight. Now he could hear the third voice, which would be that of Hamp's wife—a true constant soprano which ran without words beneath the strophe and antistrophe of the brother and sister:

"Sold him in Egypt and now he dead."

"Oh yes, Lord. Sold him in Egypt."

"Sold him in Egypt."

"And now he dead."

"Sold him to Pharaoh."

"And now he dead."

"I'm sorry," Stevens said. "I ask you to forgive me. I should have known. I shouldn't have come."

"It's all right," Miss Worsham said. "It's our grief."

And on the next bright hot day but one the hearse and the two cars were waiting when the southbound train came in. There were more than a dozen cars, but it was not until the train came in that Stevens and the editor began to notice the number of people, negroes and whites both. Then, with the idle white men and youths and small boys and probably half a hundred negroes, men and women too, watching quietly, the negro undertaker's men lifted the grey-and-silver casket from the train and carried it to the hearse and snatched the wreaths and floral symbols of man's ultimate and inevitable end briskly out and slid the casket in and flung the flowers back and clapped-to the door.

Then, with Miss Worsham and the old negroes in Stevens's car with the driver he had hired and himself and the editor in the editor's, they followed the hearse as it swung into the long hill up from the station, going fast in a whining lower gear until it reached the crest, going pretty fast still but with an unctuous, an almost bishoplike purr until it slowed into the square, crossing it, circling the Confederate monument and the courthouse while the merchants and clerks and barbers and professional men who had given Stevens the dollars and half-dollars and quarters and the ones who had not, watched quietly from doors and upstairs windows, swinging then into the street which at the edge of town would become the country road leading to the destination seventeen miles away, already picking up speed again and followed still by the two cars containing the four people—the high-headed erect white woman, the old negress, the designated paladin of justice and truth and right, the Heidelberg Ph.D.—in formal component complement to the negro murderer's catafalque: the slain wolf.

When they reached the edge of town the hearse was going quite fast. Now they flashed past the metal sign which said Jefferson. Corporate Limit. and the pavement vanished, slanting away into another long hill, becoming gravel. Stevens reached over and cut the switch, so that the editor's car coasted, slowing as he began to brake it, the hearse and the other car drawing rapidly away now as though in flight, the light and unrained summer dust spurting from beneath the fleeing wheels; soon they were gone. The editor turned his car clumsily, grinding the gears, sawing and filing until it was back in the road facing town again. Then he sat for a moment, his foot on the clutch.

"Do you know what she asked me this morning, back there at the station?" he said.

"Probably not," Stevens said.

"She said, 'Is you gonter put hit in de paper?' "

"What?"

"That's what I said," the editor said. "And she said it again: 'Is you gonter put hit in de paper? I wants it all in de paper. All of hit.' And I wanted to say, 'If I should happen to know how he really died, do you want that in too?' And by Jupiter, if I had and if she had known what we know even, I believe she would have said yes. But I didn't say it. I just said, 'Why, you couldn't read it, Aunty.' And she said, 'Miss Belle will show me whar to look and I can look at hit. You put it in de paper. All of hit.' "

"Oh," Stevens said. *Yes*, he thought. *It doesn't matter to her now. Since it had to be and she couldn't stop it, and now that it's all over and done and finished, she doesn't care how he died. She just wanted him home, but she wanted him to come home right. She wanted that casket and those flowers and the hearse and she wanted to ride through town behind it in a car.* "Come on," he said. "Let's get back to town. I haven't seen my desk in two days."

"Sold him in Egypt. And now he dead." Why do the negroes think this reference appropriate? Is there any justice in the accusations implied here?

At the end, do Stevens and the editor regret their efforts?

"Strophe" and *"antistrophe"* (page 195) are technical terms from the incantatory poetry of Greek tragedy. Are they out of place here, describing the chanting of Hamp and his sister?

The last really long paragraph, beginning "Then, with Miss Worsham", is all one sentence. How might the writer defend this construction?

You may detect in Faulkner's style a tendency to inflation, or to a very deliberate assertion of "significance"; for example "the wreaths and floral symbols of man's ultimate and inevitable end" or the repeated and stylized descriptions of the heat. If so, would you say that they help or hinder the story?

FOR FURTHER READING: The easiest approach to Faulkner is probably by the *Collected Stories* (three volumes) or by the novel *The Unvanquished*. Both are published by Chatto and Windus, and *The Unvanquished* is also in Penguins.

WALTER DE LA MARE

Walter de la Mare (1873–1956) was one of the best poets writing, both for children and adults, in the first half of this century; his short stories are less well known but often very distinguished. Much of his early writing, from the familiar children's poems to so comparatively testing and serious a work as *The Wharf*, is concerned with fantasy or dream, with the underlying and sometimes dark mysteries of the mind. This is probably the most grown-up story in this book; its honest facing of mental terror, and its refusal to be sensational, are truly adult.

The Wharf

She gave a critical pat or two to the handsome cherry bow, turning her head this way then that, as she did so; pulled balloonishly out its dainty loops; then once more twisted round the small figure with its dark little face and dancing burning eyes, and scanned the home-made party frock from in front.

"What does it *look* like, mother?" the small creature cried in the voice of a mermaid: then tucked in her chin like a preening swan to see herself closer. The firelight danced from the kitchen range. There was an inch of snow on the sill of the window, and the evergreen leaves of the bushes of euonymus beyond bore each its platterful of woolly whiteness.

"Please, mother. What do I look like?" the chiming voice repeated; "my frock?"

With that wearer within it, it looked for all the world like the white petals of a flower; its flashing crimson fruit just peeping out from beneath. It looked like spindle tree-blossom and spindle-berries both together. And the creature inside danced up and down with the motion of a bird on its claws, at sight, first of the grave intentness and ardour and love in its mother's eyes; and next, in expectation of the wonderful party, which was now floating there in the offing like a ship in full sail upon the enormous ocean.

"Then I look nice, mother, nice, nice, nice?" she cried. And her mother smiled with half-closed eyes, just as if she were drinking up a little glass of some strange far-fetched wine.

"You are my precious one," she said, still gazing at her. "And you will be *very* good? And eat just a little at a time, and not get over-excited?"

"Oh dear, oh dear," cried the mite, her dark face turning aside in dismay like a tiny cloud from the sunrise; "they won't never, never be done dressing."

"There, now, be still, my dear," her mother pleaded. "You mustn't excite yourself. Why, there they are, you see, coming down the stairs."

And when the three—the two elder fair ones and this—were safely off, she returned to the fire, knelt down to poke it into a blaze, and then reclining softly back upon her heels, remained there awhile, quite still—brooding on a distant day indeed.

Something had reminded her of a scene—a queer little scene when you came to think of it, but one she would never forget, though she seldom had even the time to brood over it. And now there was one whole long hour of peace and solitude before her. She was with herself. It was a scene, even in this distant retrospect entangled, drenched, in a darkness which, thank Heaven, she could only just vaguely recall. To return back even in thought into that would be like going down into a coal-mine. Worse; for "nerves" have other things to frighten with than merely impenetrable darkness. The little scene itself, of course, quite small now because so far away, had come afterwards. It shone uncommonly like a star on a black winter night. And yet not exactly winter; for cold wakens the body before putting it to sleep. And that time was like the throes of a nightmare in a hot still huge country—a country like Africa; enormous and sinister and black.

And so, piece by piece, as it had never returned to her before, she explored the whole beginning of that strange experience. She remembered kneeling as she was now, half sitting on her heels, and looking into a fire. A kitchen fire, then, as now; though not this kitchen. And not winter, but early May. And behind her the two elder children were playing, in their blue overalls, the fair hair gently shimmering in the napes of their necks as they stooped over their toys. It was, of course, before this house, before tiny Nell had come—dark and different from her two quiet sisters. And yet—good gracious me, how strange things are!

As now at this moment, she had been alone in that kitchen, even though the children were there. And alone as she had never been before. It seemed as though she had come to the end of things—a vacant abyss. Her husband had gone on to his work after having been with her to the doctor. She remembered that doctor—a taciturn, wide-faced man, who had listened to her symptoms without the least change of countenance, just steadily fixing his grey eyes on her face. Still, however piercing their attention, and whatever the symptoms, they could only have guessed at the horror within.

And then her husband had brought her home again, and

after consoling her as best he could, had gone off late and anxious to his work, leaving her in utter despair. She must go away at once into the country, the doctor had said, and go away without company: must leave everything and rest. Rest! She had hated the very thought of the country: its green fields, its living things, and the long days and evenings with nothing to do; and then the nights! Even though a farm was the very place in the world she would have wished to have been born in, to live in, and there to die, she would be more than ever at the mercy there of those horrors within. And country people can stare and pry, too. They despise Londoners.

The extraordinary thing was that though her husband had reeled off to the doctor, as if he had learned it all by heart, as if he wanted to get rid of it once and for all, the long list of her symptoms, the one worst symptom of all he had never had the faintest glimpse of. His pale face, that queer frown between his eyebrows and the odd uncertain way in which he had moved his mouth as he was speaking, though they showed that he was talking by rote—or rather, talking just as men do, with the one idea of making himself clear and business-like, were yet proof too of what he was feeling. But not a single word he had said had touched her inmost secret. He hadn't an inkling that her awful state, body and soul, was centred on *him*.

She could smile to herself now to think what contortions the body may twist itself into when anything goes wrong in the mind. That detestation of food, those dizzying moments when you twirl helplessly on a kind of vacant devilish merry-go-round; that repetition of one thought on and on like a rat in a cage; those forebodings rising up one after the other like clouds out of the sea in an Arabian tale. Why, she had had symptoms enough for every patent medicine there was. She smiled again at the thought of her portrait appearing in the advertisements in the newspapers for pills and tonics, her hand clutching the small of her back, or clamped over a knotted forehead.

Still, though she quite agreed now, and had almost agreed then, that it had been wise to see the doctor, and though she agreed now beyond all telling that she owed him what was infinitely more precious even that life itself; still she hadn't breathed to her husband one word about that dream; not a word. And never would. Not even if she lay dying, and if its living horror came to her then once again—though it never would—in the hope of crushing her once for all, utterly and for ever.

It was something no one could tell to anybody. There were vile things enough in the world for everyone to read and share, but this was not one even a newspaper could print, simply because she supposed no one could realize except herself how abject, how unendurable it was. Perhaps this was because it was a dream, she wondered. Dreams are more terrible than anything that happens in the day, in the real world.

A gentle quietude had descended upon her face lit up by the firelight there. It was as if the very thought of a dream had endued it with the expression of sleep. Nor, of course, was there anything to harm her now. This was yet another mystery concerning the life one's spirit lives in a dream, in sleep. The worst of haunting dreams may lose not only its poison, its horror, it may even lose its meaning, just as dreams of happiness and peace, in the glare and noise of day, may lose the secret of their beauty. Not that *this* particular dream had ever lost its meaning. It had kept its meaning, though what came after had completely changed it—turned it outside in, so to speak.

And now, since she was sane and "normal" again, just the mother of her three children, with her work to do, and able to do it—the meaning did not seem really to matter very much. You must just live on, she was thinking to herself, and do all you have to do, and not push about or pierce too much into your hidden mind. Leave it alone; you will be happier so. Griefs come of themselves. They break in like thieves, destroying as they go. No need to seek *them* out, anticipate *them*!

But what a mercy her husband had been the kind of man he was—so patient over those horrible symptoms, so matter-of-fact. It was absurd of the doctor to try to hurry him on, to get testy. Clever people are all very well, but if her husband had been clever or conceited he would have noticed she was keeping something back—might have questioned her. And then she would have been beyond hope—crazy.

And that, of course, put one face to face with the unanswerable question: was what she had seen real? *Was* there such a place? Were there such dreadful beings? After all, places you could not see had real existence—think of the vast mountainous forests of the world and the deserts and all their horrors! And perhaps after death? . . . For a while the white-faced clock on the wall overhead, hanging above the burnished row of kitchen tins, ticked out its seconds, without so much as one further thought passing in her mind. The room was deliciously warm; all the familiar things in it were friendly. This was home. And in an hour or two her husband would return to it; and a little later their three girls: the two fair ones, with the little dark creature—tired probably and a little fretful—between them. And life would begin again.

She was happy now. But thinking too much was unwise. That had really been at the root of her Uncle Willie's malady. He could not rest, and then had become hopelessly "silly"—then, his visitors! What a comfort to pretend for a moment to be like one of those empty jugs on the dresser; or, rather, not quite empty but with a bunch of flowers in one! And a fresh bunch every day. If you remain empty, ideas come creeping in—as horrible things as the "movies" show; prowling things. And in sleep, too, one's mind is empty, waiting for dreams to well in. It is always dangerous—leaving doors ajar.

And so—she had merely come round to the same place once more. But now, and for the first time since that visit to the country, she could afford to face the whole experience. It was surprising how its worst had evaporated. It had begun in March by her being just "out of sorts", overtired and fretful. But she had got better. And then, while she was going up to bed that night—seven years ago now—her candle had been blown out by a draught from the dark open landing window. Nothing of consequence had happened during the evening. Her husband had been elated by a letter from an old friend of his bachelor days, and she herself had been doing needlework. And yet, this absurd little accident to her candle had resembled the straw too many on the camel's back.

It had seemed like an enemy—that puff of wind: as if a spectre had whispered, "Try the dark!" And she had sat down there on the stairs in the gloom and had begun to cry. Without a sound the burning tears had slowly rolled down her cheeks as if from the very depths of her life. "So *this* was the meaning of everything!" they seemed to tell her. "It is high time you were told." The fit was quickly over. The cold air at the landing window had soothed her, and in a moment or two she had lit her candle again, and, as if filled with remorse, had looked in on her two sleeping children, and after kissing them, gone on to bed.

And it was in the middle of that night her dream had come. After stifling in her pillow a few last belated sobs, lest her husband should hear her, she had fallen asleep. And she had dreamed that she was standing alone on the timbers of a kind of immense Wharf, beside a wide sluggish stream. There was no moon, and there were no stars, so far as she could remember, in the sky. Yet all around her was faintly visible. The water itself as if of its own slow moving darkness, seemed to be luminous. She could see that darkness as if by its own light: or rather was conscious of it, as if all around her was taking its light from herself. How absurd!

The wharf was built on piles that plunged down into the water and into the slime beneath. There were flights of stone steps to the left, and up there, beyond, loomed what appeared to be immense unwindowed buildings, like warehouses or granaries; but these she could not see very plainly. Confronting her, farther down the wharf, and moored to it by a thick rope, floated on the river a huge and empty barge. There was a wrapped figure stooping there, where the sweeps jut out, as if in profound sleep. And above the barge, on the wharf itself, lay a vague irregular mass of what had apparently come out of the barge.

It was at the spectacle of the mere shape of this foul mass, it seemed, that she had begun to be afraid. It would have horrified her even if she had been alone in the solitude of the wharf—even in the absence of the gigantic apparition-like beings who stood round about it; busy with great shovels, working silently in company. They, she realized, were unaware of her presence. They laboured on, without speech, intent only on their office. And as she watched them. . . . She could not have conceived it was possible to be so solitary and terrified and lost.

There was no Past in her dream. She stood on this dreadful wharf, beside this soundless and sluggish river under the impenetrable murk of its skies, as if in an eternal Present. And though she could scarcely move for terror, some impulse within impelled her to approach nearer to discover what these angelic yet horrifying shapes were at. And as she drew near enough to them to distinguish the faintly flaming eyes in their faces, and the straight flax-coloured hair upon their heads, even the shape of their enormous shovels, she became aware of yet another presence standing close beside her, more shadowy than they, more closely resembling her own phantom self.

But though it was beyond her power to turn and confront it, it seemed that by its influence she realized what cargo the barge had been carrying up the stream and had disgorged upon the wharf. It was a heap, sombre and terrific, of a kind of refuse. The horror of this realization shook her even now, as she knelt there, the flames of the kitchen fire lighting up her fair blonde face. For, as if through a whisper in her consciousness from the companion that stood beside her—she knew that this refuse was the souls of men; the souls not of utterly vile and evil men (if such there were; and no knowledge was given her of where *their* souls lay or where the blessed) but of ordinary nondescript men—"wayfaring men, though fools". Yet nothing but what seemed to be a sublime indifference to their laborious toil and to its object, showed on the faces of the labourers on the wharf.

Perhaps if there had been any speech among them, or if any sound—no more earthly than echo in her imagination—of their movements had reached her above the flowing of that vast dark stealthy stream, and above the scrapings on the timbers of the shovels, almost as large as those used in an oast-house, she would have been less afraid.

But this unfathomable silence seemed to intensify the gloom as she watched; every object there became darker yet more sharply outlined, so that she could see more clearly, up above, the immense steep-walled warehouses. For now *their* walls too seemed to afford a gentle luminosity. And one thought only was repeating itself again and again in her mind: The souls, the souls, of men! *The souls, the souls, of men!*

And then, beyond human heart to bear, the secret messenger beside her let fall into consciousness another seed of thought.

She realized that her poor husband's soul was there in that vast nondescript heap; and those of loved-ones gone, wayfarers, friends of her childhood, her girlhood, and of those nearer yet, valueless, neglected—being shovelled away by these gigantic, angelic beings. "Oh, my dear, my dear," she was weeping within. And, as with afflicted lungs and bursting temples she continued to gaze, suddenly out of the nowhere of those skies, two or three angle-winged birds swooped down and alighting in greed near by, covertly watched the toilers.

And one, bolder than the rest, scurried forward on scowering wing, and leapt back into the air burdened with its morsel out of that accumulation. The sight of it pierced her being in this eternity as if that morsel were her own. And suddenly one of the shapes, and not an instant too soon, had lifted its shovel, brandishing it on high above his head, with a shrill resounding cry—"Harpy!"

The cry shattered the silence, reverberated on and on, wharf, warehouse, starless arch, and she had awakened: had awakened to her small homely bedroom. It was bathed as if with beauty by the beams of the nightlight that shone on a small table beside her bed where used to sleep her three-year-old. It was safety, assurance, peace; and yet unreal. Unreal even her husband—his simple face perfectly still and strange in sleep—lying quietly beside her. And she—lost amid the gloom of her own mind.

Tell *that* dream—never, never! But yet now in this quiet firelight, so many cares over—and, above all, that dreary entanglement of the mind a thing of the past—what alone still kept the dream a secret was not so much its horror, but its shame. The shame not only that she should have dreamed such a dream, but that she should as it were have seen only its horror and had become its slave.

To have believed in such a doom; to have supposed that God. . . . But she could afford to smile indulgently now at this weakness and cowardice and infidelity. She could afford it simply because of Mr. Simmonds, the farmer. That was the solemn, the really-and-truly amusing truth. It was that rather corpulent, short, red-faced Mr. Simmonds who had been responsible for the very happiest moment in her life: who had saved her, had saved far more even than her "reason".

Her husband, of course, knew how much they owed to his kindness. But he did not know that he owed Mr. Simmonds her very heart's salvation, if that was not a conceited way of putting it. And yet it was this Mr. Simmonds—she laughed softly out loud as she gazed on into the fire—it was this Mr. Simmonds who had at first sight, in his old brown coat and mud-caked gaiters, reminded her of a potato! Of a potato and then an apple, one of those cobbled apples, their bright red faded a little and the skin drawn up. His smile was like that, as dry as it was sweet, like cider.

What an interminable Sunday that had been before her husband and the two children had said good-bye to her at the railway station. How that man in spectacles had stared at her over his newspaper. Then the ride in the trap, her roped box behind, and Mrs. Simmonds, and the farm. Two or three times a day at least she had rushed out in imagination to drown everything in the looking-glass-like pond among the reeds not very far from the farm. And yet all the time, though Mrs. Simmonds knew she was "queer", she could not possibly have guessed, while she was talking to her of an evening in the parlour, the things that were flaring and fleering in her mind like the noises and sights of a fair.

The doctor had said—looking at her very steadily: "But you won't, you must remember, be really much alone, because you will have your home and your children to think of. You will have *them*. Think as little as possible about everything else. Just rest, and be looked after."

The consequence of which had been the suspicion that she

was being not merely "looked after" but watched. And she would openly pretend to set out from the farm in another direction when she was bent on looking once more at her reflection in the pond. None the less she had remembered what the doctor had said, had held on to it almost as if it had been a bag she was carrying and must keep safe. And by and by in the hayfields, in the lanes by the hedges, she had begun to be a quieter companion to herself and even glad of Mrs. Simmonds's company, and of talking to her plump brown-haired daughter, or to the pale skimpy dairy-maid.

It was curious though that, while passing the opening in the farm-wall she had never failed to cast a glance towards that dark distant mound with its flowers beyond the yard, she had never really noticed it. She had seen it, even admired its burden, but not definitely attended to it. It had taken her fancy and yet not her eye. She had been far less conscious of it, for example, than of the pretty Jersey heifer that was sometimes there, and even of the tortoiseshell cat, and the cocks and hens, and of the geese in the green meadow.

All these she saw with an extraordinary clearness, as if she were looking at them from out of a window in a strange world. They quieted her mind without her being aware of it, and she would talk of them to Mrs. Simmonds partly because she was interested to hear about them; partly to keep her in the room; and partly so that she might think of other things while the farmer's wife was talking. Of other things!—when first and foremost, like a huge louring storm-cloud on the horizon of a sea, there never left her mind for a single moment the memory and influence of her dream. It would sweep back on her, so much distorting her face and clouding her eyes that she would be compelled to turn her head away out of the glare of the parlour lamp, in case Mrs. Simmonds should notice it.

And then came that calm, sunlit afternoon. She had had

quiet sleep the night before. It had been her first night at the farm untroubled by sudden galvanic leaps into consciousness and by the swarming cries and phantom faces that appeared as soon as her tired-out eyes hid themselves from the tiny radiance of the nightlight.

She had been for a walk—yes, and to the reed-pond—and had there promised her absent husband and her two children never to go there again unless she could positively bear herself no longer. She had promised; and, quieted in mind, she was coming back. She remembered even thinking with pleasure of the home-made jam that Mrs Simmonds would give her for her tea.

There was no doubt at all, then, that she had been getting better—just as before (when the dream came) she had been really, though secretly, getting worse. And as she was turning in home by the farm gate, she saw Nellie, the heifer, there; the nimble young fawn-haired creature, with its delicate head and lustrous eyes with their long lashes; and she had advanced in her silly London fashion, with a handful of coarse grass, to make real friends with her. The animal had sidled away and then had trotted off into the farmyard, and she had followed it with an unusual effort of will.

The sun was pouring its light in abundance out of the west on the whitewashed walls and stones and living creatures in the yard; midges in the air, wagtails, chaffinches in the golden straw, a wren scolding, a cart-horse in reverie at the gate, and the deep black-shadowed holes of the byres and stables.

Still eluding her, Nellie had edged across the yard; and it was then that, lifting her eyes beyond the retreating creature, she had caught sight of that mound, now near at hand, and had realized what it was. She had realized what it was almost as if her dream had instantly returned with it, almost as if the one thing were the "familiar" of the other. But the horror now was more distant. She could not even (more than vaguely, like reflection in water) see those shapes with the shovels simply because what she now saw in actuality was so vivid and lovely a thing. It was a heap of old stable manure; and it must have lain there where it was for a very long time, since it was strayed over in every direction, and was lit up with the tufted colours of at least a dozen varieties of wild flowers. Her glance wandered to and fro from bell to bell and cup to cup; the harsh yet sweet odour of the yard and stables was in her nostrils: that of hay was in the air; and into the distance stretched meadow and field under the sky, their crops sprouting, their green deepening.

And as she stood, densely gazing at this heap, she herself it had seemed became nothing more than that picture in her eyes. And then Mr. Simmonds had come out and across the yard, his flannel shirt-sleeves tucked up above his thick sunburned arms, and a pitch-fork in his hand. He had touched his hat with that almost schoolboyish little gentle grin of his; then when he noticed that she was trying to speak to him, had stood beside her, leaning on his pitch-fork, his glance following the direction of her eyes.

For a moment or two she had been unable to utter a syllable for sheer breathlessness, and had turned her face aside a little under its wide-brimmed hat, stammering on, and then almost whispering, as if she were a mere breath of wind and he a dense deep-rooted oak tree. But he had caught the word "flowers" easily enough.

There must have been at least a score of varieties on that foster-mothering heap; complete little families of them: silver, cream, crimson, rose-pink, stars and cups and coronals, and a most marvellous green in their leaves, all standing still together there in the windless ruddying light of the sun. And Mr. Simmonds had told her a few of their country names, the very sounds of them like the happy things themselves.

She had explained how exquisitely fresh they looked—not

like street-flowers though she supposed of course that to him they were mere waste—just "wild" flowers.

And he had replied, with his courteous "ma'ams" and those curiously bright blue eyes of his in his plain plump face, that it was no wonder they flourished there. And as for being "waste", why, they were kind of enjoying themselves, he supposed, and welcome to it.

He had been amused, too, in an almost courtly fashion at her disjointed curious questions about the heap. It was just "stable-mook"; and the older that is, of course, the better. It would be used all right some time, he assured her. The wild flowers, pretty creatures, wouldn't harm it; not they. They'd fade by the winter and *become* it. Some were what they called annuals, he explained, and some perennials. The birds brought the seeds in their droppings, or the wind carried them, or the roots just wandered about of themselves. You couldn't keep them out of the fields! That was another matter. You see there you had other things to mind. And with that charlock over there! . . .

And still she persisted, struggling as it were in the midst of the dream vaguely hanging its shrouds in her mind, as if towards a crevice of light to come out by. And Mr. Simmonds had been patience and courtesy itself. He had told her about the various chemical manures they used on the crops. That was one thing. But there was, she gathered, what was called "nature" in *this* stuff. It was not exactly the very life of the flowers, for that came you could not tell whence, it is the "virtue" in it. It and the rain and the dew was just as much and as little their life-blood—their sap—as the drink and the victuals of humans and animals are. "If you starve a lad, ma'am, keep him from his victuals, he don't exactly flourish, do he?"

Oh yes, he agreed such facts were strange, and, as you might say, almost unknowledgeable. A curious thing, too, that what

213

to some seems just filth and waste and nastiness should be the very secret of all that is most precious in the living things of the world. But then, we don't all think alike; "'t wouldn't do, d'ye see?" Why, he had explained and she had listened to him as quietly as a child at school, the roots of a tree will bend at right-angles after the secret waters underneath. He crooked his forefinger to show her how. And the groping hair-like filaments of the shallowest weed would turn towards a richer food in the soil. "We farmers couldn't do without it, ma'am." If the nature's out of a thing, it is as good as dead and gone, for ever. Wasn't it now the "good-nature" in a human being that made him what he was? That and what you might call his very life. "Look at Nellie, there! Don't her just comfort your eye in a manner of speaking?"

And whether it was Mr. Simmonds's words, or the way he said them, as if for her comfort—and they were as much a part and parcel of his own good nature as were his brown hairy arms and his pitch-fork and the creases on his round face; or whether it was just the calm copious gentle sunshine that was streaming down on them from across the low heavens, and on the roofs and walls of the yard, and on that rich brown-and-golden heap of stable manure with its delicate colonies of live things shedding their beauty on every side, nodding their heads in the lightest of airs; she could not tell. At that very moment and as if for joy a red cock clapped his wings on the midden, and shouted his *Qui vive*.

At this, a whelming wave of consolation and understanding seemed to have enveloped her very soul. Mr. Simmonds may have actually seen the tears dropping from her eyes as she turned to smile at him, and to thank him. She didn't mind. It was nothing in the world in her perhaps that he would ever be able to understand. He would never know, never even guess that he had been her predestined redemption.

For a while they had stood there in silence, like figures in a picture. Nellie had long since wandered off, grazing her way across the meadow. She had now joined the other cows, though she herself was but a heifer, and had not yet calved or given milk. How "out of it" a Londoner was in country places! Her very love of it was a kind of barrier between herself and Mr. Simmonds.

And yet, not an impassable one. Knowing that she was "ill", and being a "family man", and sympathetic, he had understood a little. She had at last hastened away into the house; and shutting her door on herself, had flung herself down at her bedside, remaining there on her knees, with nothing in the nature of a thought in her mind, not a word on her lips; conscious of no more than an incredibly placid vacancy and the realization that the worst was over.

The kitchen fire had lapsed into a brilliant glow, unbroken by any flame. Her lids smarted; she had stared so long without blinking into its red. She must have been kneeling there for hours, thus lost in memory. Her glance swept up in dismay to the clock; and at that instant she heard the scraping of her husband's latch-key in the lock—and his evening meal not even so much as laid yet!

She sprang to her feet and, stumbling a little because one of them had "gone to sleep", met him in the doorway. "I am late," she breathed into his shoulder, putting her arms round his neck with an intensity of greeting that astonished even his familiar knowledge of her. "But there were the children to get off. And then I just sat down there by the fire a minute. Jim: don't think I'm never thankful. You were kind to me that time I was ill. Kinder than you can possibly think or imagine. But we won't say anything about that."

Her arms slipped down to her sides; a sort of absentness spread itself over her faintly lit features, her cheeks flushed by the fire. "I've been day-dreaming—just thinking: *you* know.

How queer things are! Can you really believe that that Mr. Simmonds is at the farm *now*, this very moment?" Her voice sank lower. "It's all snow; and soon it will be getting dark; and the cows have been milked; and the fields are fading away out of the light; and the pond with the reeds. . . . It's still; like a dream—and now. . . ."

And her husband, being tireder than usual that afternoon, cast a rather dejected look at the empty table. But he spoke up bravely: "And how did the youngsters get off? They must have been a handful!"

He smoothed her smooth hair with his hand. But she seemed still too deeply immerged and far-lost in her memory of the farm to answer for a moment, and then her words came as if by rote.

" 'A handful'? They *were*—and that tiny thing!—I am sometimes, you know, Jim, almost afraid of those wild spirits —as if she might—just burst into tiny pieces some day—like glass. It's such a world to have to be careful in!"

This is a story of great gentleness with great force. If you have found it unrewarding, or too puzzling, first re-read the descriptions of the Wharf, page 206, and of the "midden" or muck-heap, page 212. These are the heart of the story.

Notice that de la Mare begins and ends with the youngest child, Nell, who was still unborn at the time of the mother's nervous illness, and is "dark and different from her two quiet sisters". By the time Nell was born her mother's experience, of horror and of revelation, was far deeper. The last paragraph of the story hints again at this idea.

Any clichés about "nervous breakdowns", or half-baked psychology, are useless here; for the mother's ordeal and recovery are made inward for us, refusing to be simplified into a classification, and we are reminded, as in THE RAIN

HORSE, *how much of our experience is still mystery. Some interpretation can be attempted, however. It may be worth noting that the image of the Wharf, and the sluggish river, recalls slightly the ancient Greek idea of the rivers of the Underworld, which a man's soul was forced to negotiate. More important, we should notice that it is not herself but her husband the woman is mainly concerned for; her deep love for him underlies the whole story; and the horror of the Wharf is not simply that of mortality, but that of the indifference which the weird labourers show towards the "refuse" of souls, and of the scavenging Harpy which snatches a soul (Jim's?) away.*

Against, and above, this dream is set positive and vital good. The family happiness, the child's eagerness at the beginning; the brilliant and delicate farmyard life, and Nellie, the beautiful young heifer which leads the way to the midden (perhaps the youngest child is named after her); above all the midden itself, representing in its richness of flowers the complete cycle of living and dying, decay and fertility: these are all written of with an intense and careful joy. Of all the stories in this book this is the one which sends us most grateful, most appreciative, back to life; and this is literature's highest function.

FOR FURTHER READING: Any volume of poetry by Walter de la Mare. *Best Stories of Walter de la Mare* published by Faber and Faber.

ACKNOWLEDGEMENTS

Acknowledgements are due to the following for permission to include stories in this anthology:

To Messrs. J. M. Dent & Sons Ltd., and the Trustees of the Dylan Thomas Estate for permission to use a slightly edited version of *The Peaches* by Dylan Thomas; to the Society of Authors as the literary representative of the Estate of the late Katherine Mansfield for *Her First Ball* by Katherine Mansfield, and as the representative of the literary trustees of Walter de la Mare for *The Wharf*, by Walter de la Mare; to Messrs. Jonathan Cape Ltd., and the Executors of the Ernest Hemingway Estate, for *Indian Camp* by Ernest Hemingway, from *The First Forty-Nine Stories*; to Messrs. Jonathan Cape Ltd. for *Ha'penny* from *Debbie Go Home* by Alan Paton; to Messrs. Faber and Faber Ltd. and the author for *The Rain Horse* by Ted Hughes from *Introduction*; to Messrs. Faber and Faber Ltd. and the author for *The Wedge-Tailed Eagle* by Geoffrey Dutton from *Australian Stories of Today*; to Messrs. Hamish Hamilton Ltd., and Mrs. James Thurber for *The Secret Life of Walter Mitty* from *The Thurber Carnival*, this story originally published in the *New Yorker*, © 1939 James Thurber; to Messrs. Macdonald and Co. Ltd. for *The Road* from *Collected Stories* by James Hanley; to Messrs. Michael Joseph and Curtis Brown Ltd. for *Growing Up* from *Spring Song* by Joyce Cary; to Messrs. Chatto & Windus Ltd. for *Lie Thee Down, Oddity!* from *God's Eyes A-Twinkle* by T. F. Powys, and for *Go Down, Moses* by William Faulkner; to Messrs. Rupert Hart-Davis Ltd. for *Samphire* from *Lying in the Sun* by Patrick

Acknowledgements

O'Brian; to Laurence Pollinger Ltd. and the Estate of the late Mrs. Frieda Lawrence for *Tickets, Please* from *The Complete Short Stories of D. H. Lawrence* published by Messrs. William Heinemann Ltd.; and to Messrs. The Bodley Head Ltd., for *The Ice Palace* from *The Bodley Head Scott Fitzgerald Volume 5*.